ALONE

WITH THE

STARS

ALONE
WITH THE
STARS

BOOK THREE OF THE
STAR STITCH CHRONICLES

Hazel Vale

HAZEL VALE BOOKS

First published by Hazel Vale Books

Ontario, CA

hazelvalebooks.com

Book cover design by moorbooksdesign.com

Inside formatting by Hazel Vale Books

Edited by Stephanie Hollingsworth - Lilac Editing Services

ISBN: 978-1-7780882-5-4 (paperback)
ISBN: 978-1-7780882-4-7 (ebook)

For Charlotte
Always be yourself and never be afraid to yell potato.

And for any reader wearing an invisible corset
I hope you get your breath back.

One

Lady Lucy studied her uncle's hair. The ashy sweep curled like a frozen wave. She imagined small spiders surfing the wisp, coasting from one side of his head to the other.

The grand ball had ended mere minutes before, and Lucy had been summoned to the study for yet another lecture.

Avoiding his steel-blue gaze, she let her focus wander from his hair to his expertly tailored black dinner jacket. Crimson points on the collar flared like raven wings dipped in blood.

In contrast, Lucy's copper gown resembled an autumn forest, giving her a soft fairy-like look. Rich brown lace billowed out of the high slit in her skirt, complementing her blond hair. A string of glittering citrine gems pulled the matching lace of her sleeve to a point and stretched it over her copper-tipped middle finger.

The gown had been designed especially for this ball by Wynter Canmore, who was now the most sought-after seamstress in the hex-system. It was perfection, marred only by Wynter's reluctance to remain and watch Lucy dancing in it.

Like everyone else, Wynter had left.

"Are you listening to me?" Lord Daye asked. His face had begun to match his trim.

"Not really."

"Your stunt at tonight's ball made it impossible to introduce you to Lord Blackwell. I thought we'd agreed that his family's Idex was perfect and that he would readily accept an offer of marriage."

The stunt he referred to involved Lucy shepherding a small flock of infant lambs into the ball. As hostess, she thought it was a delightful touch to the evening. Upon minimal reflection she had to admit that lambs at a ball may not have been her most successful idea; there was the smell and noise, of course, and the fact that they lacked any regard for where they relieved themselves.

The Valtine aristocracy reacted with an unprecedented abundance of shock and horror. If the lords and ladies of the Valtine court feared the adorable balls of fluff, perhaps they shouldn't be in charge of things. Or if she had made such a blunder—which she wasn't convinced she had—perhaps she shouldn't be future heiress to the largest land title in the entire hex-system.

The past months had been a grand display of Valtine control and opulence. Valtine exerted heavy influence over the other hex-system planets, from Orion to Corva, not to mention the outer planets, moon bases, and satellites.

With such a vast scope of power, it was a wonder anyone else thought themselves significant.

Even with all of the benefits of being born with the right Idex on the right planet, they still required constant entertainment to remind themselves of their rank and importance. Her uncle had paraded her around to ensure they accepted her as an equal; he was determined that she be in a position to make a marriage offer to a Valtine lord. An offer Lucy had never—not once—agreed to make.

They were now at Silva Castle, the Daye forest estate. Spires and turrets flanked the smooth, dark stones stacked four stories high. Polished opal, sapphire, and gold inlaid every curve and doorframe. And hidden behind the frames was a scanner for everyone's Idex: an organic compound that was passed down through the maternal line. It was traced, tracked, and updated throughout the hex-system.

Guests could barely move without her uncle knowing where they were. It was a castle engineered for control.

Lord Daye continued to rant, his strangled voice filling the room he'd specifically chosen for tonight's lecture. He was getting close to an embarrassingly unfashionable yell. Lucy moved away and took a few unhurried steps to cross the room. Burgundy and ink-black swirled papers plastered the walls. Swords hung from diamond-shaped holders between jewel-studded shields.

Every fourth section, a quiver with feathered arrows was anchored beside a decorative longbow. The bows had been out of use for far too long and weren't in functioning order. Lucy knew they didn't maintain them regularly because she had tried shooting one of them the day before. She had nocked the arrow and drawn back. The strong silver fibre had held, but the carved wooden limbs had creaked with each pull. Before she could even take aim at the mustard-brown sitting chair (that most certainly deserved to be shot at), the tension on the dried wood had caused it to crack, splinter, and shatter.

An empty spot on the wall was hard to miss, as was the broken bow that now poked out from under the dais.

Lucy rubbed her forehead. She was getting weary and felt ready to sleep. It had been an eventful evening, and she was tired of Lord Daye's constant lectures. She was never good enough—not even close to acceptable. In the year since her aunt's disturbing disappearance, she'd proven to be an inadequate replacement.

Lucy wanted to go home to Orion, to her father and the guilds. But her uncle had contrived a way to control her every movement, making escape impossible.

He stormed across the room to where she was pushing a row of books back from the edge, leaving an uneven line of dust on the shelf. He grabbed her arm and gave her an abrupt shake.

"What's the point in talking to you if you aren't hearing a word I say?" Lord Daye roared, finally losing all control.

"I really don't know; I was wondering the same thing myself."

A lamb bounced into the room and released a perky bleat. Lucy spun on her heel, pulling her arm out of her uncle's grasp. She picked up the lamb and stroked its soft wool, then turned back to face her uncle's rage.

Lord Daye had never been a violent man. He considered displays of anger far beneath him: but in that moment, Lucy was almost afraid. He was holding his breath like a child. His face had taken on an unusual shade of pink, and he balled his hands into fists.

Lucy wisely took a step toward the open door.

"If you refuse to see the seriousness of this situation, then you force me to take more drastic measures."

Lucy was well aware of the seriousness of the situation. The high level of control the Valtine courts exerted on the other planets was creating resentment over the Idex system of rank and the ever-widening cracks gave voice to dissenters. Lady Daye had gone missing at the worst possible time. She was Lucy's father's sister, which meant they did not share an Idex. Idex bloodlines were ancient. Everyone was born with one inherited from their mother, and only the maternal line was ever recorded. But as Lady Daye's only living relative, and with an Idex almost as ancient, Lucy was still in a position to inherit her aunt's lands.

Unrest simmering between the planets was increasing.

Cracks were forming everywhere. And for some reason, her uncle thought a marriage to Lord Blackwell was going to fix everything. He was obsessed with the idea. As far as Lucy could tell, he had vastly underestimated the problem if he thought a marriage could save them.

No, she was well aware of the seriousness of the situation—she simply didn't care. Just as she didn't care that masquerade masks shouldn't have feathers or horns. Or that fast reels were now allowed at a midweek ball. Or that cake should not be stirred into haze. She didn't care that it was improper to thank the butler who seamlessly cleaned up the champagne she had intentionally spilled. The only thing she cared about was finding her way home. And not marrying Lord Blackwell or any other Valtine lord who would force her to stay on this dreadfully boring planet.

Two

The lamb wiggled in Lucy's hold and let out a timely bleat, calling farewell to Lord Daye as he pushed past her and stalked out of the room.

Lucy waited a minute before following him out.

All around, she heard the sounds of the evening being cleared away. Each room needed to be reset and made ready for the morning. After weeks of planning, it was all over in such a short time.

"You wouldn't make me marry a boring old lord, would you?" she asked the lamb, nuzzling it against her cheek.

Lucy considered bringing the lamb to her room, but her cat, Nix, was unlikely to accommodate another guest, and the small creatures had made a considerably large mess.

Her dancing shoes padded softly on the marbled floor as she made her way toward the back of the castle. She smiled at the two maids carrying bundles of fresh flowers and nodded at any lingering guests who wandered the halls instead of retiring for the night.

Spiral stairs brought her to a back entrance that led to the gardens and stables.

The evening was warm and rich. Trees towered overhead, letting in slivers of moonlight. The silver roof of the stables marked the edge of the castle walls that hedged in the forest beyond. Blue lights shone up from below the honeycomb-shaped stone path. Four large buildings housed horses, chickens, and the lambing pens.

The smell of hay and fresh oats greeted her as she neared the pen.

The moon slipped out from behind the clouds, brightly illuminating the footpath. Rounding the corner, she stumbled back and nearly dropped the lamb as she collided with the tall man leaning against the wall.

His unbuttoned evening shirt showcased his well-toned muscles and the iron lantern hanging above his head cast him in a favourable light. His blue eyes shone, his tousled hair gave him a rakish air, and a half grin revealed the dimple on his left cheek. She had to admit he possessed a devilishly handsome charm.

"Lord Ryon, what are you doing out here?"

She liked Lord Ryon, who was a bit of a flirt and rarely took anything seriously. His very presence annoyed her uncle, which she also liked.

He pulled away from the wall and swayed a little as he took a step in her direction. She remembered he'd had a bit more haze than most at the ball and had stepped on the edge of her gown more than once when dancing.

"Lucy—did you come to dance with me again?" he asked. He swayed side to side and hummed a tune only he could discern, making a large circle with his arms that invited her to join him.

Lucy giggled. Hazed or not, he remained charming.

"No, of course not—I have a lamb to return." Lucy held the lamb as it bleated and wiggled. She leaned over the half-open door and put the lamb in its pen.

In the time it took to put the lamb down, Ryon had come up behind her. The open shirt put his chest dangerously close to her. Heat rushed to her cheeks.

"One last dance, before you're consigned to Lord Blackwell."

Lucy bristled at the mention of that name. She knew Lord Daye expected her to make an offer of marriage within the next moon, and he'd apparently not wasted any time sharing the expected news with the rest of the court.

"Don't pout; I didn't mean any offence. I know it's not your fault." He leaned in, brushing aside a stray blond hair.

A shiver of delight tingled up her arms. She looked back at Lord Ryon, scrunching her nose and narrowing her eyes as she studied him intensely. They had grown up attending some of the same functions, as his family often visited Orion.

Perhaps he was the sort of man she would marry if given the chance.

"Now that the lamb is gone, won't you dance with me?" he asked merrily, then grabbed her arm and pulled her in so she'd be in step. "Your hair is like golden moonlight, and you look like a woodland fairy who's stepped out of my dreams. Won't you dance with me, high goddess of the night? For one moment, stoop down to the mortal realm."

She smiled at his ridiculous compliments and wondered if her hair really glowed in the moonlight. It probably did, with all the sprays and gels Josephine had put in her hair to keep it in place—it probably glowed even without the moonlight.

He leaned in, as if he had forgotten about dancing and might attempt to kiss her. His warm breath mixed with the overpowering stench of haze.

Lucy wrinkled her nose and leaned away.

As much as she enjoyed his attention, she had no interest in kissing him. She took a half step back until she was pressed against the barn wall.

The hanging light swayed in time with him, illuminating his slack smile.

He laughed a tune. It wasn't a pleasant laugh; it was cold and mean. He suddenly felt much taller.

"I think it's time you go to bed," she said, poking a finger right in his chest and immediately regretting the touch to his clammy skin. She pushed slightly, and he rocked back a little, widening the distance between them.

He closed his eyes. Lucy wondered if he'd fallen asleep. She ducked under his arm and collided with yet another wayward lord.

He was more dishevelled than Lord Ryon and lacked the charm. Hard, grumpy lines had turned his face sour. He stumbled past her, barely acknowledging her presence, held up a bottle of haze, and slapped Ryon on the back.

"Sorry, you swept me off my feet—ah, Trive! Wasn't trying to kiss you now, was I?" Lord Ryon asked.

Lucy let out a sigh of relief. She needed only to scream and a dozen servants would have come running, but there were some types of attention Lucy wasn't fond of.

Thankfully, the two of them didn't notice her as she slipped away into the night.

Through the labyrinth of stairs and halls, Lucy made her way back to her suites.

Open veranda windows let in the evening breeze. Steam rose from the large black stone tub in the middle of the room. Water slowly flowed over the edge into a moat and ran down to the veranda, where it spilled like a waterfall into the lake beyond her window. Silky curtains hung from the ceiling and drew around the tub.

A nightdress hung from the nearby garment rack. Josephine had thought of everything. She fought with the laces of her dress until her fingers cramped, pulling the body of fabric to her side to pop open the buttons, then wiggled, jumped, and clawed her way out of the dress. She should have called for Josephine, but the girl must be exhausted. Free from her dress, she threw it on the floor and sank into the tub.

Her lady's maid, Josephine, was a constant bright spot amid the lengthy stay. Josephine had dreamed of seeing Valtine. Her Idex lacked the status required to be employed on the planet, but Lucy, born on Orion—a fact many tried to ignore—had found a loophole by enlisting Josephine as her personal help.

Some of the staff had objected, but no one had the will to argue for long.

Nix meowed, letting Lucy know she'd been soaking long enough.

After a lazy attempt at drying off, the remaining drops of water seeped into her dressing gown as she flopped into her bed. The orange cat pawed at her still-damp hair, reminding her she'd done a terrible job of drying herself, and then snuggled up beside her.

Lucy stared up at the ceiling, wondering if Lord Ryon and

Lord Trive would end up passing out in the lambing pens, or if Lord Blackwell had seen her bring lambs into a ball. Consumed by a longing for home, she gave herself over to homesickness for a moment before banishing her troubles and falling asleep.

Three

Lucy slept well past lunchtime. Josephine woke her, trying to hide the red and swollen eyes peering out from under the black hair that framed her heart-shaped face. She looked as though she'd been crying for longer than a few minutes.

"Jo—what's wrong?" Lucy asked, sliding out of her bed without disturbing Nix.

"It's cancelled. Everything. All our trips. Lord Daye has told everyone to pack up. He says you're leaving," Josephine sobbed. She uncrumpled a square bit of fabric and dabbed at her eyes.

"Leaving? No. We just got here. We can't be going already," Lucy said, knowing Josephine must have misunderstood. Lord Daye had dragged her all over Valtine from one location to the next, but they'd always stayed a full moon. Lucy had almost hoped her uncle would give up on her and leave her here. Silva Castle was quiet when they weren't hosting an event. It was out of the way—and a perfect place for him to ignore her existence.

"I've been told I can't come. I don't know where they're

going to send me." Josephine darted to the enormous wardrobe at the far end of the room and flung open its wooden doors. She stood with her hands at her sides, staring hopelessly into the chasm of dresses.

Before Lucy could figure out how to counter Josephine's distress, a brief knock sounded, and then a small army of smartly gowned women entered the room. They all wore their hair in tight braids curled at the base of their necks. The low buns looked itchy. Lucy rubbed the back of her neck and contemplated how many pins would be needed to keep the buns in that precise location. They wore white blouses with puffed sleeves tucked into floor-length soft-pink skirts. Round bobbled earrings hung from their ears. The scent of roses followed them into the room, and Lucy half expected them to sing. But they remained silent except for the faint sound of breathing. None met Lucy's eye.

Poor Josephine looked down at her own day dress in horror. She wore something of a woodland-green uniform, similar to their surroundings. Blue fish swam up the trim, and a smart, flowing skirt billowed to her ankles. Lucy knew Josephine had loved it when she'd picked it out. It would be a shame if the lively dress caused her to feel self-conscious now. She scurried back to Lucy and tucked herself up beside her.

"They can't make you leave," Lucy said, patting Josephine on the hand and trying to console her.

"Yes, they can, and they are. *She's* coming. If I ever see you again, you'll be like them," Josephine whispered.

If the row of women overheard her, they did a perfect job of pretending not to.

Lucy was not as easily distressed as Josephine and released

her hand. She stood and stretched in her flimsy dressing gown. She was barely awake and was not in the best mood to entertain maids who'd made her friend so uncomfortable.

Crossing the room, she perched on the edge of the tub, letting her fingers tickle the top of the water as her foot dangled above the floor.

A cool breeze swept in from the open veranda. The trickle of the waterfall and rustle of leaves was overshadowed by the sharp clip of heels on stone. The newest arrival to the morning party was a middle-aged woman who looked quite average at first glance. A deep-purple dress flattered her fit frame. There was no severe bun; instead, rich brown hair curled in perfection over her shoulders. The curls were pulled back from her forehead, making it look larger than it should have. Like a glassy lake, her face lacked any sign of a wrinkle, as if she never smiled or frowned.

The army of ladies took a single step back, letting the woman pass by and approach Lucy.

"Stand up, I want to look at you," the woman commanded.

"I think you can see me just fine." Lucy's stomach rumbled, and she hoped this wouldn't take too long.

"I am here for you, so there is little point in refusing my dictates. My name is Evost Stone. I am not a lady or a companion or a guest or a staff member. You are to follow my every instruction. I am called in for young women—to train them."

"I am not young," Lucy responded automatically. The way Evost said *women* made Lucy shudder, as if she took sole credit for birth, life, and everything after by simply imparting instructions. Lucy may have grown up on Orion, but she'd heard plenty of stories about women like this, mostly from her friend Lady Cristelle and others who had grown up among the Valtine court. It was a fate her father had spared her.

"No—not young, but Lord Daye has decided it is necessary to have you re-educated. These ladies will wait on you to ensure you are dressed and presentable enough to catch the right attention." Turning, Evost faced Josephine and—much to the young maid's evident horror—addressed her directly. "You are dismissed."

Josephine's face went white, her eyes wide with unshed tears.

Lucy rolled her eyes. She was officially annoyed at Evost. Anyone could see the maid's distress. There was no need to be so cold. "Josephine, dear, I'm terribly hungry. Would you mind finding me something for breakfast?"

Josephine looked from Evost to Lucy, then back again. She hurried from the room. Lucy hoped she would take her time—poor thing.

"It's because of the lambs, isn't it?" Lucy hopped down from the edge of the bath, letting her nightgown drop to the floor. Fresh undergarments waited for her, and she stepped into them and donned the first layer of a simple blue gown. The soft slip fit tightly to her chest and fell down over her hips. She tugged a little on the bottom so it lay flat against her skin and hung halfway to her knee.

Evost said nothing, but waited patiently—at least she looked patient.

It was hard to tell.

Evost took a small datapad from a waiting maid and handed it to Lucy. On the screen was a contract signed by Lord Daye, granting Evost authority. But if Lord Daye had been unable to bend Lucy to his will, she wasn't concerned about whatever control Evost thought she could muster. She was a grown woman, capable of making her own decisions.

"Let's make a truce, of sorts. I'll go along with this re-education—for now—and promise to do my very best, and you let Josephine stay on Valtine." Lucy put the datapad down as if it carried little importance to her.

"Deal," Evost replied too quickly. The ladies snapped to attention, and Evost started giving orders.

Gowns were pulled in a flurry from off the floors and out of racks and drawers. Black travel trunks arrived.

Evost was quickly saying yes and no, and items were swiftly packed.

Before Lucy could protest, a silver corset was placed around her waist. She had always liked the look of a corset, but found them much too confining—although this one did have an intriguing look that she liked. The shine of tech reminded her of the hull of the Obsidian. She was thankful for the soft layer of blue she wore underneath. The corset had some give but forced her to stand straight in order to catch a full breath.

"Oh, I think you've set it a mite too tight," Lucy gasped. She heard a series of electronic closures seal into place. The soft silver fabric pulled in without putting pressure on anything major. But it was tight.

Wordlessly, the ladies draped a travelling dress over the corset and laced it up the back, while others continued packing her things. What was usually a lengthy ordeal took a matter of minutes.

"Oh Lucy, what did you agree to?" Josephine cried as she rushed back into the room. A light wooden platter with handles sat balanced between her hands. Thankfully, there were lids on all the glasses, keeping the sloshing coffee and other various treats contained.

"Nothing. Lord Daye did all of the agreeing for me. But don't worry, I made a deal, and you can stay on Valtine," Lucy replied more calmly than she felt. Her stomach rumbled, and she reached for the coffee.

"But I don't want to stay on Valtine, that's what I tried to tell you. They're taking you away," Josephine sobbed.

Evost watched the exchange with a smirk. It was the closest thing to a facial expression so far.

Lucy had made a deal in order to keep Josephine on Valtine and walked right into Evost's plans.

"The Nova-Manor arrived yesterday. Lord Daye has decided it is time to take a break from hosting and to show you the inner workings of the Valtine court."

Lucy had never seen the Nova-Manor, but everyone in the hex-system knew of it. The mansion of a ship had an extraordinary reputation. It was more of a resort home than a spaceship and would circle the planet and slide between the moons, offering the best views of Valtine. It was for parties and politics.

She looked to Josephine, who radiated fear. She wished she could reassure the girl that it would all be fine, and that it would only be for a few weeks. It would help Josephine enjoy a more relaxed stay on Valtine while Lucy was gone. Perhaps once she arrived she could find a way to have Josephine brought up. There was always a way to get what she wanted eventually.

Lucy took the lid off her coffee, breathing in the comforting aroma as she sipped the swirling black liquid. Nix, who'd finally woken, purred and rubbed his back against Lucy's leg, unconcerned with the surrounding chaos.

"I'm not sure if I need to mention it, but that thing won't be coming," Evost said. "Josephine's continued employment will include caring for the creature while you're away."

"The deal we made was for Josephine to be allowed to stay on Valtine. I said nothing about leaving Nix behind." Lucy couldn't count the number of times she'd been told Nix could not come with her. Fortunately, Nix was great at space travel.

The ladies' maids finished packing her trunks in record time and were already moving them out of the room. Evost appeared unconcerned with Lucy's defiance, repeated that the cat would not be coming, and continued to make demands on everyone around her.

Lucy had heard dozens of stories about hired women like Evost; even Lady Cristelle had endured some form of training. But Lucy was a highly ranked adult heiress—how much could Evost truly require of her?

Lucy took another long drink of coffee, tugged on her travelling coat, and eyed Evost warily. Lord Daye had clearly decided he no longer wanted to deal with her and had passed her off to Evost as a project—perhaps this was a good sign that he was weakening and giving up. Maybe when Evost reported back that it was a hopeless case, she would be free to return home. Maybe it would all work out in her favour.

The look on Josephine's face suggested that her maid felt otherwise.

Four

Goodbyes were difficult. It would only be for a few weeks, but they had both cried. Mostly Josephine.

Lucy encouraged her to take some time to enjoy the forest and the estates, and to relax. There were certain perks to being a lady, and Lucy had been able to install Josephine in her private rooms while she was gone. Someone had to watch over her dresses, and apparently no one saw fit to question Lucy about it. Josephine was her responsibility, after all.

After being fed, Nix crawled into his carrier. It looked like a normal bag any lady would carry, but it provided enough room for him to sit comfortably. Somehow, he always knew to remain quiet.

Aside from not being able to bring Josephine with her, Lucy was looking forward to being on the Nova-Manor. The manor was the size of a sprawling castle, and she was certain she could avoid Lord Blackwell. Unlike Silva Castle with its endless Idex tracking, the Nova-Manor was reported to have none—or at the very least, a minimal amount. It's what gave it the reputation of being a ship designed for politics. One could talk freely or have secret meetings without every interaction being recorded by the host.

Lord Daye would despise the lack of Idex tracking.

Lucy boarded the small shuttle with a dozen other excited women. She recognized the ladies Sophia and Zandra, Holly, and Blithe. They giggled and talked to each other. They were much younger than she was and only in their first year, they all came from good families, with titled lands and hopes to make a match. They wore various shades of blue, rose, and green travelling jackets, all with fashionable white buttons and rows of pearls over the shoulders. Lucy usually got along well enough with them all, but as soon as they saw her, they stiffened and lost all of their previous enthusiasm. Gone were the bright eyes and wide smiles.

Lady Zandra lifted a hand to offer a wave, but Holly pulled it back down.

"You know the rules," Holly said sharply.

Zandra pressed her lips in a straight line and stared forward.

Lucy sighed but wasn't going to let their lack of communication get her down. She would survive Evost and whatever she had planned, and then life would go back to what it had always been.

The shuttle took off, leaving the beautiful castle behind. As they neared Nova-Manor, the group of ladies broke from their forced calm and strained to look out the window. The nearing ship looked like a moon cut in half, sitting on a long, arrow-shaped platform. Iridescent gold shutters partly covered the glass dome. The other half was open, and they could see the top deck. Pools, trees, and shingled huts dotted the port side; a narrow river snaked through the middle. The moving people looked like bits of blown confetti from so far away.

For a moment, the girls forgot whatever secrecy had stopped them from speaking to her. Desperation mingled with excitement as they chatted about finding husbands.

"I'm the last of my sisters to be married. I have four older sisters, and so I barely have a dowry—and my eldest sister already has two daughters. There's nothing for me but a good match," Zandra said, resting her chin on her hands.

Lucy couldn't relate. While the ladies across from her had an abundance of sisters but limited inheritance, she possessed an infinite inheritance with little family. She wondered how many children her parents would have had if her mother had not died.

They docked, and the shuttle doors opened. Trollies lined the dock, waiting for the massive trunks and packages. Lucy held Nix's case close to her chest, making sure no one tried to take it from her.

Men in snow-white suits waited to escort them. Lady Zandra let out a sweet giggle, wiggled her arm into the crook of the waiting concierge, and flashed a dazzling smile at the others.

They walked in pairs down the halls. Black floors burst with swirls and sparkling strands of silver. Wispy silver lines reached up the walls and spread like tree branches, covering the parts of the ceiling that weren't open to the stars above.

Nova-Manor was truly a unique perfection.

One by one, the young ladies were dropped off at their rooms.

Lucy peeked past one woman to see an enormous bed, cushioned couches, lounge chairs, and a wood desk with a wall-length mirror.

"Evost would like you to come this way," her escort said. He cleared his throat uncomfortably.

She followed him away from the girls, down a lift, and arrived two floors below. It was quiet and cozy. The same black and silver swirls followed through, but the walkways were narrower and the doors closer together.

They stopped in the middle of the hall. Her escort was unable to hide his nervousness as he opened her door.

A large window trimmed in black overlooked a conservatory. A solitary pillow adorned the plain grey blankets that covered the small bed. An equally sparse washroom adjoined the bedroom.

The escort hurriedly left, and Evost Stone appeared.

"You have your own bathroom. Your dressing rooms are across the hallway. I will be choosing your wardrobe. The gowns will be simple and elegant and more traditional than the over-the-top nonsense you have been wearing."

"My Aunt Daye wore whatever she wanted," Lucy said, unconcerned. She knew she looked fantastic no matter what she wore.

"Your aunt is not here—and this is the last time you will mention her. I am trying to distance you from that scandal as much as possible. You must appear stable."

Lucy had a retort ready, but Nix, who was still in his bag, moved. She shifted it and set it on the bed, then quickly stood in front of it, folding her hands.

"Yes, of course. I understand," Lucy said dutifully, hoping Evost would leave before Nix gave himself away.

Evost nodded smartly.

"You will be down for dinner promptly. You're allowed to discuss your new surroundings as well as simple issues pertaining to Valtine—like the lavender fields' yield this year."

As soon as the door closed, Lucy opened the bag and let Nix out. Unclipping the bottom compartment, she watched as the compact cat case unfolded with a compressed bed, food bins, and box. She took out a round container of food and set it on the floor. She moved her bed away from the wall just enough to set everything up behind, hiding his new home from view. Nix brushed against her ankles as she worked then pounced on her feet. Lucy scratched Nix behind the ears, then left him to explore his new living quarters. She went across the hall to her dressing room to get ready for what sounded like an incredibly dull evening.

Of all the choices, Evost had laid out an unfortunate sallow-green gown for her to wear. It fit well. Soft peridot gems adorned the neckline. There was nothing terrible about it, except that it was nothing. It was a dress meant for someone to glance right over. Lucy shifted in her corset, already annoyed by its restrictions.

At dinner, Lucy noted that most of the young ladies had been strategically placed near a potential husband, but not so close as to solidify any matches. Lucy sat between two matronly women, with two ladies on either side of them, and a bench of women across from her. As Lucy was there for Lord Blackwell alone, it seemed Evost did not think she was ready to meet him yet.

Lucy leaned back in her chair to peruse the other tables. At least three hundred men decorated the room, and she only recognized a few. If Lord Blackwell was among them, it would be impossible to figure out who he was. Although she knew the type who was usually seen in her uncle's company. They were always much too old for her. Lord Blackwell could be any one of these self-important-looking men who appeared to be waiting for someone to make a mistake to prove their own superiority.

Lord Ryon talked animatedly two tables over. She caught his eye and lifted her hand to wave. The corset pulled a little, and she winced. Lord Ryon winked at her, and she rewarded him with a blush. Lady Blithe across the table sent her a daggered look and flicked her eyes warningly toward where Evost sat, watching Lucy's every move.

Dinner progressed slowly, each portion of food delivered on gold plates and topped with useless garnishes.

Lucy sighed. She was so bored she wanted to cry. No one could possibly be enjoying themselves. Little things stuck out to her. The way Lady Blithe pretended to chew long past finishing in order to avoid conversation with Lady Filla. The way Lady Filla told the same story three times. It concerned a deer she'd seen, but she failed to elicit excitement from anyone else over the event. The way Lady Susan spoke so quietly that no one knew what she'd said, and no one ever bothered to ask her to repeat herself.

Dessert arrived, and Lucy counted the seconds, hoping the end was near. She stirred the bland ice cream in her bowl, then picked a few of the flowers from the table centrepiece and added them to the swirl, watching them melt into the cream as it liquified. Rescuing the drowning petals, she floated them on the top, arranging them into a frowning face. She tilted it toward Lady Holly on her left, who let out a giggle.

When the evening finally ended, a footman informed Lucy that she would not be dancing, and he escorted her back.

The maids waiting for her unpinned her hair in silence. They brushed her long blond hair down her back and washed the hint of makeup off her face.

Evost shadowed the door.

"I can't wait to get out of this corset and have a long, hot bath," Lucy said, addressing the maid who was helping her and ignoring the pesky phantom at the door.

"You will do neither. You can sleep in the corset for the night, and perhaps the discomfort will make you think about how you behave."

"If I have an uncomfortable sleep, then I'll look dreadful tomorrow."

"Then you won't leave your room until you've recovered. Perhaps this will teach you to follow the rules which I clearly lay out."

"I don't remember there being any rules about what I do with my ice cream."

"What did you do to your cream?" Evost said, showing the first signs of exasperation. Lucy realized her mistake when she noted the small red scratch, like a crimson thread, darting across Evost's perfect hand. Lucy looked past her, across the hall and into her open room.

Apparently, not even her room was her own. Since she saw no sign of Nix, she assumed he'd gotten away. Nix could take care of himself, but Lucy would miss his presence.

"Perhaps this will teach you to stay out of my room," Lucy retorted. Before she could leave, two of the maids came up behind her and reset the coil controls on the corset. Trying to take a full breath, Lucy expanded her lungs and pushed against the silver cage.

Evost almost smiled, then left.

The maids said nothing and did nothing to ease her pain.

"Well, I'll see you all in the morning," Lucy said cheerily and pirouetted in the hallway before slamming her door and collapsing on her bed.

Lucy was already bored of this game and Evost needed to be stopped.

Five

The white ceiling had no distinguishable lines, cracks, swirls, or imperfections. Lucy lay on her back on the hard mattress, squinting through the light of her small lantern. Her lungs pressed against the corset, unable to get a full breath.

This was nothing short of torture.

A band around the bottom made it impossible to get her fingers underneath the edge, and every attempt to stretch the fabric made things worse.

Lucy tried to reach the panel at the back, but the sealed cogs kept her out. The strong silver material held her in tight, permanently creasing the folds of her blue underdress.

She was suffocating and needed to get out.

Now.

Searching her room took less than a minute. The side table had a small coil lantern and no other decorations. She found no clothing, no pictures on the wall. Not even a hanger or pen to assist her.

She pulled the perfect white sheet off her bed, folded it in half, and wrapped it around her body twice. The bunched edge tucked neatly into the top, holding it fast. The sheet hung a little low on the left side but wasn't worth fixing.

Lucy opened her door, thankful Evost hadn't resorted to locking her in. Perhaps she thought it unlikely Lucy would venture out without a dress on. Evost had seriously underestimated her.

Ghostly shadows slipped up and down the empty hall. A silver spire of light twinkled inside the decorative handheld lantern. She took a moment to look down the hallway and back, half expecting Evost to be standing guard.

Without a plan, she trotted down the hall and around the corner, following the ever-brightening lights. She reached the end as it darted off in four directions. A spiralled black post in the middle of the intersection reached from the floor to the ceiling. Above her head, illuminated signs pointed the way to the pools, the hedge maze, the theatre, and the study.

If the study was decorated like Silva Castle, she would get lucky and find the walls covered with all manner of weapons and pointed objects. Taking the wide hall, she wound her way through the labyrinth of passages. At the end of the long tunnel of doors, she reached the study. An open book was carved on the door, set in silver and surrounded by trees, moons, and ancient writings. Lucy ran her hand over the cool metal with all its bumps and grooves and wondered who had made such an extraordinary door. Had they enjoyed their labour, or was it one of hundreds that they'd tired of?

After a moment of reflection, she entered. Her sheet-dress caught the edge of the door, threatening to disrobe her. Lucy stumbled, grabbed at the fabric, and pulled it tight, tucking it back in.

Holding her lantern high, she walked down one wall, illuminating dozens of locked bookshelves. A pang of longing hit her fiercely, taking away the little breath she had. An entire wing at her Orion home was dedicated to books. Her mother would have loved this place. After she'd passed, her father had continued collecting. He'd laid books two deep until the Orion library overflowed the shelves and spilled into hallways. Unlike these books, which were perfectly tucked away, her family's collection was open for anyone to take from and read. Lucy gave herself a moment to hold the memory, the longing—she let it wash over her. Letting the memory pass, she continued her search for something sharp.

Lucy's bare feet were cold on the floor. The shelves kept going and going. It wasn't a cozy study at all, but an enormous tomb. High-backed chairs and small round tables floated like individual islands throughout the room. If cleared, the study could host a grand ball.

When she reached the very end, she held up her lantern and saw her deliverance. Between two of the shelves, hanging from the wall, was a tall iron sconce. It was scrolled, and the top came up to a sharp point.

The decoration didn't move when she pulled on it. She tried to lift, slide, push, and pull, but it didn't even wiggle in place.

Her mind spun, searching for other options, but if it was so securely fastened, perhaps it might be used in another way. If she could get the tip under her corset and pull, surely the fabric would tear.

Resolved, she dropped her sheet, set her lantern on the floor, and backed up until the sconce touched her. She raised herself up on her toes. The pointed tip didn't even come close to the bottom of her corset. Realizing she'd misjudged its height, Lucy picked up her lantern and searched the room for the nearest end table. Dragging it over, she stood on it, her bare feet clammy on the polished finish.

It was a little higher than she needed. With her knees bent, she caught the pointed tip and slid it under the corset. The iron scraped a long line up her back, barely fitting between the skin and the fabric. A small price to pay if this worked.

Taking a shallow breath, she kicked the end table away, letting her full weight hang until the air rushed out of her in a sickening gust of breath. She kicked her feet like a puppet. The corset slid up and pinched into her armpits until she felt as though her arms were going to rip off.

The stubborn fabric didn't tear or let go. It held her weight, dangling her on the wall.

The swirl of her lantern on the floor illuminated her toes, casting dancing shadows that were soaked back into the darkness. Lucy wondered what would happen first: whether she'd be suffocated, or have her arms fall off. Her head pounded, and she let out the tiniest cry.

A stream of cuss words thundered from the far side of the study. A chair scraped across the floor, then heavy footfalls echoed through the room. She heard another cuss as someone banged into the end table in the darkness.

The little light by her toes was engulfed in a black mass as someone stepped over it, plunging her into darkness.

She tried to say something, but the words came out as an odd squawk. Strong hands wrapped around her waist. He held his hands still for a moment, applied a little pressure, then adjusted how he gripped her, spanning her side. In one swift move, he hoisted her off of the wall.

Her relief was short-lived. Lucy tried to inhale the moment her toes hit the floor, but the corset had tightened. It mattered little that they were in darkness. She could feel the inky black specks as they formed in the corners of her eyes. Her head swam, and she knew she was close to passing out.

This was worse than when she'd first tried to get the wretched corset off.

The lantern was uncovered and picked up. Before she could see who held it, the mysterious man turned her so she faced the wall. Fingers wrapped around her wrists, the lantern dangling from his thumb, and he raised them against the wall above her head, giving her room to take in tiny sips of air.

"Try to hold still." His voice was low, and his breath hot against the back of her neck. She heard the unmistakable sound of a blade flicking open. Every second dragged on as the extra pressure on her spine burned where the spike had dug in.

With one hand, he slowly opened the sealed panel. The silver fabric pulled in, and then a slow release let the corset fall open.

Lucy could breathe.

The knife clicked closed, and echoed in the silence.

Holding the corset with one hand, he slid it out from around her and released the hands he still had pinned above her head.

The heat from his nearness dissipated as he stepped back.

Lucy rested her head against the wall, listening to his journey across the study. She let a few tears of relief fall before bringing her arms down and finally pushing away.

Without her lantern, she searched around in the dark for her white sheet. She slung it over her shoulders like a half torn cape.

She'd been rescued off the wall by a mysterious man who'd left her without a lantern. But she could breathe.

Her fingers dusted the floor, finding nothing.

He had also taken her corset.

Six

The glow of the lantern gave off very little light. A faint flicker in the hollow room cast a dark, spooky glow.

When she finally reached him, she knew why she'd missed him before. His tall chair was one of three, all angled toward the blackened windows.

This was an odd situation, even for her. Evost herself wouldn't have known the appropriate etiquette. Corset thief at midnight did not make the approved list of conversations.

She waited a few minutes for him to say something.

When he didn't, she took three steps closer toward his chair.

With two more steps, she stood beside him. Kicking the unfolded sheet out from under, she sat on the chair to his left and folded the fabric over her almost-bare legs. Thank goodness for the blue slip she'd had the sense to put on before the corset.

"Aren't you going to ask me what I'm doing?" he asked. His voice was unfamiliar. If she'd met him before, she didn't know him well enough to recognize his voice. A deep amber robe hooded his features. The corset lay over his legs, the panel open and the small light illuminating a control panel. The inner workings of her corset looked more like a flattened ship than a garment.

She could make out his jawline and his hands as they worked. A knife flashed like lightning between his fingers as he opened a miniature coil. He adjusted something, then closed it back up. His hands were not a worker's hands, and despite his cursing, he held a formal manner.

For a moment… the way he handled the blade… she wondered if he was Jasper—that is, Lord Terrington. That man had been lurking around since Lady Cristelle left, and Lucy had noticed his habit of fidgeting with a knife. But it couldn't be him. Jasper had picked up an odd sort of accent, which only happened from being among the outer planets for too long. This man sounded very much like a Valtine lord.

"What are you doing?" Lucy finally asked, leaning forward. She couldn't see his face from under the cloak without getting too close and practically sticking her head under his hood.

"I'm fixing your corset."

"I don't think I want it fixed. I'd rather not wear it at all." Lucy wrinkled her nose and sat back in the chair, less interested in what he was doing.

"How long will you have before Evost finds out you're not wearing it and puts another one on you?"

Lucy pondered the fear for a moment, wondering why Evost would have a second when she'd made the first one so difficult to escape from.

"Do you think she has an entire trunk of corsets?"

"I know she does."

"How do you know so much about women's garments? It's not a usual topic of conversation among the gentlemen of the Valtine court."

"How do you know I'm from the court?"

"Oh, knowing you're part of the court is easy. But how do you know Evost is the one who gave me the corset and that I didn't fall into it on my own?"

"I have sisters, and I recognize her work."

The answer was plausible and annoyingly vague. Most of the young men in attendance had land-titled mothers and sisters.

"Are you being intentionally elusive or protecting me from your identity?"

"Perhaps I'm protecting myself. If news of this got out, it would cause quite a scandal."

It probably would—but nothing Lucy wasn't used to. She couldn't blame him for wanting to keep his identity a secret. Silence stretched for a few minutes while he worked. Lucy shifted uncomfortably. He wasn't unkind, but he also wasn't exceptionally forthcoming, either. His tone hinted at annoyance, but maybe it was because he'd been sitting in the dark—alone—before being interrupted.

"What did you do to earn a corset like this?" he asked, not once looking up.

"I brought lambs into a ball." Lucy threw out the half-truth, hoping it didn't change his mind. The air in the room cooled, and he shifted. Lucy noted the tension even in the darkness.

"Why?"

"I was bored." Lucy ran her hands over the edges of the large chair and squinted in the darkness. Maybe he would agree with Evost once he knew the reason.

He seemed to ponder her answer for a moment.

"Boredom doesn't fully explain lambs."

"I love lambs,"

"Which could also be true, but is that the full answer? Do people just believe your boredom reached a level requiring lambs? Or that you simply had an affinity for the animal?" he asked pointedly.

Yes, of course they did. Pretending to be silly and flighty was an art form she'd mastered.

No one ever questioned her excuses. She was intrigued and genuinely wanted to know what he would say if he knew the truth, and so she gave it to him.

"If you really want to know, my uncle planned to introduce me to someone I did not want to meet. I do not want to marry him, or any other Valtine lord, for that matter. Lambs were the most reasonable option."

"I see."

"You're not going to question whether it was the most reasonable way to prevent an introduction?"

"When talk of marriage is involved—in those circumstances, ladies often have little in the way of reasonable options. And so, lambs may have been the best course of action. Do you not want to marry?"

Yes, she thought, someday she wanted to get married. But lately she'd been told so often that no one would want to marry someone like her—and she didn't want to marry a Valtine lord—that it seemed like a silly dream at present.

"Only if he has green eyes and wears golden slippers to bed. Besides, all the men on Valtine are far too old for me," she responded.

"Old? There have to be dozens—hundreds of eligible men."

"Lord Ryon is probably the closest to acceptable, but he drinks too much. And age isn't always measured in years."

"What do your parents have to say about this situation?"

"I try to send regular communications to my father on Orion, but he has more important things to concern himself with."

She didn't mention her mother, who had been ill for all of Lucy's memories and had passed when she was only seven. Her father, Alarik, never remarried, and the two of them lived alone in a castle full of people. They were always close, but he'd seemed almost relieved that Lord Daye had taken charge of the situation and brought her to Valtine. For her father, the complications were not limited to his sister's disappearance. They also included a guild issue with a fraudulent dressmaker and more than one murder to cover up—Lucy did not mention any of these details. "And so I am stuck on a planet that cares little for me. I find the rules beyond ridiculous. And I am so bored with it all. What *are* you doing?"

"I'm adjusting the settings on your bindings. They'll set to whatever Evost demands and then will slowly relax to the further limits to which I've adjusted them."

Silenced, Lucy's eyes widened like an electrocuted owl. She leaned closer, watching him.

"Are you enjoying your time on Valtine? Aside from corsets, of course," he asked, continuing the conversation as if his actions were completely normal. If he noticed how little she'd said, he let it pass.

"*Enjoy* isn't the word I would use. There are many pleasant things: the purple moons and the lavender fields. I enjoy hosting, and the staff are wonderful. Josephine, my maid, is having a wonderful time—but I find myself lonely. Josephine is my only real companion, and she's not allowed to attend balls or anything. We are living completely separate lives, which is a loneliness of its own. Lord Daye ignores me for the most part. He sends orders through others unless I need a direct lecture. I've been introduced to a hundred people, but few will talk to me for more than a few minutes. This is probably the longest conversation I've had with anyone. Although a mysterious stranger in the dark certainly is a highlight for other reasons."

"Shall I introduce myself?"

"Please don't. I'd rather not know who's playing with my undergarments. I'm not sure I could look you in the eye afterwards."

His hands stopped moving, but he clearly had not finished. He was thinking, and Lucy did not want to halt his progress.

"I'm sorry I interrupted your solitude," she blurted to fill the void.

"Are you?" he asked, another question she hadn't expected.

The soft leather of the chair felt smooth as she ran her fingers over the edge, looking for any bumps or ripples and trying to think of something clever to say back.

"For myself, no. But now that I am grateful for you, I feel the smallest hint of guilt that I intruded on your quiet."

He chuckled. It was low and smooth, like rippling water, putting her at ease. "I spend much of my time in silence—I can handle the distraction. I'm surprised Evost would bother with someone of your age. Stand up."

She stood to face him and realized he must have known who she was or he could not have commented on her age. The lambs must have been the giveaway. She should have asked his name, but held back.

It was more fun not knowing.

"Turn around."

She did.

He lifted the caped sheet from around her shoulder and discarded it over the chair. He was being completely proper, or as proper as one could be alone in the dark fixing corsets. But there was something delightfully uncomfortable about the way his hands rested on her hips. It sent a shiver down her spine, and a flutter filled her stomach. In the minimal light, he secured the corset in place, smoothing the material as he went, as if he'd done it a hundred times. He latched the coils, clicking them into place. They tightened, and she gasped. He counted under his breath. Then, as promised, the cogs slowly let go. She found she could breathe and move easily.

"It's not wise to loosen it any more than this," he said.

"It's perfect. Thank you." Lucy stretched and leaned from side to side. She turned, his hands still resting lightly on her hips. He mechanically pressed the sides to make sure they fit the way they should.

The lantern hung low between them, and she couldn't make out any of his features.

"Well, this was the oddest evening I've ever had. If I were retelling this to Lady Cristelle, she would certainly expect me to say you are supposed to kiss me. Unless you are married. Is that why you were alone in the dark?"

Lucy stopped her ramble, and her face flamed. She hadn't

meant to say the kissing part out loud, but she was flustered, and the moment the idea of a kiss came into her head, it hopped out.

"I'm not married, but I'm afraid I am much too old for you."

"You can't be that old."

"Age isn't always measured in years." He tossed the words back at her and removed his hands from her hips. "But so you are aware, this has been the most intriguing night I've had as well."

"That can't be too hard. You sit alone in the dark." Lucy said, heat rushing to her cheeks.

"Yes, something I should get back to."

He handed her the sheet and the small lantern that illuminated her toes, then sat back down.

"Thank you," Lucy said quietly, and slowly made her way through the chairs, annoyed that she failed to come up with a good reason to go back.

Seven

Lucy turned the wrong way a dozen times before reaching the hallway to her room. Once inside, she flopped onto her bed. She listened without moving, hoping to hear the soft signs that Nix had returned, but clearly he had found more comfortable accommodations for the night.

Closing her eyes, she replayed each moment in perfect order—wishing she hadn't been so terrified and unable to breathe when he'd taken her off the wall; wondering at how he'd stayed in the shadows and how he'd sat in the darkness, resetting her corset.

She took in a glorious, deep breath, knowing she could withstand all of Evost's particular tortures, and wished she could do it all again. But this time, she would ask questions about him. He'd been alone in the dark and had no plans to encounter her. Sleep took her as she thought up all the different ways that evening could have gone, and how wonderful it had been.

Morning broke, and the light in the hall turned into a warming glow, heralding the coming day on Nova-Manor.

Every castle, every ship, had its own way of adjusting to the change in time. Lucy knew many ladies who struggled with each move. She had done it so many times, she found it best to sleep as long as needed and stay awake as much as possible when she wasn't tired.

Evost had no reason to wake her so early but strode boldly into her room.

Lucy pulled a pillow over her eyes, blocking out the light. She wanted to stay in bed and dream about the (probably) handsome man who had rescued her.

The blankets were stripped off and tossed on the ground.

"How very unkind." Lucy frowned at her blankets. She stretched, then remembered to pretend her corset was tight and took a shallow breath. Lucy wondered what sort of woman ended up taking a job torturing young ladies. "Do you like your employment?"

Evost pursed her lips. "There is a satisfaction in being needed and doing a job no one else can do."

"If you're looking for satisfaction, you're not likely going to find it with me—I'll do my best, but I honestly think we'd both enjoy the next few weeks a little more if we did away with the corsets and early mornings. I can see by the look on your face that would be a no."

"You will be in the dressing room in five minutes," Evost commanded.

Unsure why she needed five minutes, Lucy followed her out immediately. She sat down in the green dressing chair and spun toward the set of gold-trimmed oval mirrors.

Evost glared at her reflection.

Neither was certain who had won that round.

Refusing to give any ground, Evost barked a series of orders to the waiting maids, then hurried from the room.

Instead of doing Lucy's hair right away, a maid commanded her to stand. Another took off her corset and helped her out of the dressing gown.

Plunging into a freezing bath woke her up instantly. She didn't do ice baths often, and despite the shock, she didn't entirely hate it, as she was probably meant to. The cold water woke up every sensation in her body, and it would improve her tired eyes.

The maid gave her an apologetic grimace, but Lucy didn't mind—and she made sure to let them know. She leaned her head back, letting the icy chill sweep up her neck and slink into her hair.

Home—it hit her again. The mountain paths that led to icy ponds. Her father, Viceroy Alarik, had loved the tradition and had commissioned heated pools to soak in after the icy plunge. Her resolve hardened as she soaked—there was no way she would ever marry a Lord and live on Valtine. She would not become part of this never-ending charade.

Once out, they dried her off and corseted her without saying a word.

"Do you know what Evost might like as a gift?" Lucy asked the maid, who faltered with the clasps.

"Sorry, miss—we aren't allowed to talk," she replied in a whisper.

Lucy nodded, messing up the first attempt at braiding her hair. "No matter, I enjoy talking. I can talk enough for all of us. The only person who can talk more than I can is Lady Cristelle. She can spin a story much better—mostly because I don't quite get to the end before another idea pops into my head. You know, I love this shade of lilac. It's soft and looks nice with my blond curls, don't you think? Will I be allowed to have curls? Certainly I would since it's so in fashion right now. I love your ringlets. They frame your face so nicely—oh, don't worry—I know you appreciate the compliment even though you can't say anything. How dreadful it must be to work for Evost every day. If you worked for me, we'd go shopping and out for lunch, and I'd let you try on all of my gowns, and I'd even sneak you into a ball. I did that with dear Josephine once. She was terrible at it. Got all flustered every time someone spoke to her. It didn't help that my father recognized her. He wasn't cross—but said to not do it again. I miss home. Uncle Daye says I can't go home because I'm to take Lady Daye's place (although I'm not supposed to mention her name because we're all trying to forget she disappeared), and I'd blame my uncle for her untimely departure, but he had remained on Valtine and everyone saw her on Orion before she vanished. Well, I'm lovely—you've all done an exceptional job, but I must say, I look quite fine when I first wake up too. With or without my gowns, it doesn't matter much to me. Thank you dearly, and I can't wait until we're able to visit again."

Lucy wondered if they were biting the insides of their cheeks to keep from smiling. They must be, or be sucking on sours to keep those lips in such a straight line.

Evost returned the moment they finished readying her, as if she'd counted the exact number of minutes it would take to finish. The bitter woman held a bit of a mystery, and Lucy was curious to see if there were any cracks in her scaly armour.

Lucy had many friends who wore the same stoic expression out of fear or self-protection. But Evost didn't come across as someone who was afraid or needed protection. She looked as though she enjoyed herself.

"You are to spend the day in quiet contemplation. Take compliments and say as few words as possible."

"I don't know what that is going to accomplish." They walked down the hall in the opposite direction she'd gone the night before.

"You talk too much."

"Says who?"

"Your future husband—I can assure you."

"Do you like grapes?"

"Excuse me?"

"They're an odd fruit, don't you think, the way they have a little skin that pops with juices when you bite into it? You look like someone who would like grapes."

Evost ignored her question, but Lucy knew she must be contemplating grapes as they walked. Once they reached the common areas, Evost blended into the growing crowd and disappeared. Lucy wondered if she would pounce the moment she stepped out of line.

Lucy followed the other guests until she reached the open lawns she'd seen from the shuttle.

In a moment, she forgot all about the rules or pretending to have trouble breathing.

The Nova-Manor was stunning. Some guests were playing cards, mahogany tables displayed games and dice, and hundreds of long cushioned chairs lined every pool. Flowers bloomed in large pots between black marble paths. It felt sunny and warm, like a tropical island with a black canopy above them. It was hard to believe they were in orbit, floating around Valtine.

Ambassadors were easy to pick out from the crowd, with their distinguished scarves and pinned tassels. Ladies wore everything from fancy day gowns to soft, billowing pants. Lucy wanted a pair of the soft pants in navy, with stars dancing down the sides. The fashion was stunning, and there was not a fast-trim in sight.

Lucy sat on a chair, enjoying a cup of tea and scones and watching them all. They moved like horses on a carrousel. Around and around, visiting, gossiping, and making connections. She recognized only a few of the guests. Lord Daye remained absent from the gatherings, and she wondered if more important lords were meeting in other rooms. Time passed quickly. The entire day had a magical quality, and she almost forgot about Evost.

When evening set in, she returned to her room to be redone for the night's live performance in the grand theatre. She loved music, even though she didn't have a musical bone in her body —she couldn't even hum all that well.

"How did I do?" Lucy asked Evost who had entered to preside over the room. Lucy flopped onto the chair instead of a careful movement and earned a glare. The ladies worked in perfect precision, taking everything off, only to redress her. The excessive help was no doubt meant to make her feel like a child in complete dependence. But Lucy had no problem accepting the help—she'd had it in one form or another all her life. She was more than capable of doing things for herself, but didn't need to prove that to anyone.

"How did you do?" Evost asked, irritation lacing her words. "Do you really have to ask that? Today was supposed to be simple. Just don't talk too much."

"I didn't say a single word for over two hours!"

"You were doing charades, getting everyone to guess what kind of animal you were." Evost's tone sped up the rate at which the maid hurriedly pulled pins from Lucy's hair. Lucy winced at the sharp tug.

"Oh yes, did you see how much fun everyone had? I dare say, though—my hippopotamus was dreadful—Lord Cornfred suggested I resembled an alligator with a broken tail, thankfully… "

Evost snapped a band over Lucy's hands, bringing an immediate sting. Lucy shook her hand and suppressed a smile—she must be winning if Evost was already losing control over her temper.

"Fine—no more charades. But just so you are aware, everyone enjoyed it."

"They were laughing at you!" Her control slipped, and her tone darkened. "Have you no respect for yourself? You behaved like a fool."

"At least they were laughing."

"Get her ready… and tighten it so she can't eat." Lucy stood and turned so they could reach the cogs.

The young woman's eyes widened, but Evost stood over her as her corset pulled in tighter and tighter.

"Oh, please don't," Lucy begged dramatically. She held her breath for a minute as they helped her into her evening gown. Off-white sleeves blended into a pale-blue dress—acceptable and boring. A row of pearls encircled her neck. She looked sweet and pretty. The style wasn't terrible, but it didn't suit her.

She did her best to hold still as the corset returned to its comfortable level of containment. Concealing her lack of discomfort, she remained silent and slightly subdued until the maids finished.

Eight

Lord Daye looked like a peacock, but not in a terrible way. When he walked the perfectly fitted blue suit hinted at plum undertones. Silvery-blue and deep-green trim embellished the collar and cuffs. His tamed hair lacked the plume she recalled from the last time they spoke.

Without saying a word, Lord Daye looked her over and nodded approvingly, then tucked her hand into the crook of his arm and guided her down the hall, following the signs for the theatre and the ever-growing crowd.

Everyone wore a fabulous display of crowns and jewels. Diamonds and smokey quartz towered in curls; rubies dripped down arms. Her gaze took in everything from large stones to tiny clusters of glitter.

Lucy was elegantly but woefully underdressed.

The theatre was stunningly simple and not overly adorned or fussy. Black beams arched above her head and came to a point, shooting out lines like a burst of dark fireworks. The fronts of the box seats were sparkling silver with no additional decorations. Comfortable black high-backed chairs and a polished railing held in the occupants.

It explained the fashion… everyone stood out in a flash of colour.

Lady Daye would have loved this—and she would have worn all black.

Lucy smoothed her own boring dress before sitting down. She looked soft and quiet. It felt as though she were lying to everyone by wearing it.

She leaned forward on the railing and peered at the guests below. Like private clusters in a public room, even the floor seats were a box of sorts. Four chairs remained empty in their box. "Is anyone else joining us?"

"Not this time. I realized I should take a softer approach to introducing you to society. At least you will know whom you are speaking with before you start blundering. This is my world, and it will one day be yours."

She didn't mind him telling her about everyone and how they were connected. People and connections fascinated her. Like a little web with drops of dew, they were all tied together. And like a web, equally fragile… and sticky… people were sticky.

Lord Daye wasted no time in pointing out the one man she did not want to know better.

"The man in the booth right across from us is Lord Blackwell. As you can see, he's not as old as you keep suggesting he is. I expect you to note whom he is sitting with and whom he is paying attention to."

Lucy squinted at the man across from her. Lord Blackwell didn't look old, as her uncle had said, but he had a blank expression. The almost-frown reminded her of the one Evost wore. The formal navy suit had triple folds across the front. He blended in as well as she did. She now understood the need for the simplicity of her gown.

He was unremarkable. She probably never would have picked him out of a crowd.

She pitied the women sitting around him; however, it was a fantastic display of fashions. Lady Zandra sat on his left and three others beside her. Catching Lady Zandra's eye, she smiled widely. Light-blue crystals glowed over the young lady's navy gown and cascaded down her arm. They glittered and shone under the lights.

Lord Daye pointed out other prominent families from the Valtine Court. They all looked simple and pleasant enough— unfortunately, they all had to be so prim and proper all the time. It was too bad—they might enjoy each other's company if they tried.

The orchestra started, and the curtain lifted. Lucy leaned her elbows on the railing and cupped her chin. She glanced over at Lord Blackwell and swore she saw him scowl right at her, and she remembered the corset should be too tight for her current position.

As the lights dimmed, she leaned back into her chair; any attempt to inspect the other attendees vanished.

Nova-Manor put on a fantastic show, although a little stiff. When the performance ended, they all rose from their individual boxes and crushed into the halls behind. Lucy had no intention of going back to her room or staying with her uncle.

"Thank you for the company. What a lovely evening," she said, then graciously kissed him on his cheek, surprising him enough to slip away.

Lucy pressed through the crowd, going the wrong way, thinking she might go back to the study. She waved to Zandra, who smiled and then glanced away. Lucy followed her gaze to where she spied Evost in the crowd—and ran directly into Lord Ryon. He caught her arm and kept her from stumbling.

His attire for the evening was certainly impeccable. There was a moment of jealousy that he could wear the deeply embroidered jacket, but it gave way to a blush as he wrapped an arm around her waist. Pressing the corset into her side uncomfortably, he led her to the edge of the moving throng. His eyes were bright and clear, and he thankfully didn't smell of haze.

"Darling," he murmured against her ear. He held her hand up and twirled her around. "You look absolutely terrible this evening." Lucy giggled and swatted him away.

"I didn't know you'd be here. I've been so bored," Lucy said joyfully. The way his hand had pressed into the corset... and then, as he kissed the inside of her wrist... she wondered if he was telling her something. She tried to conjure the memory of the mysterious man's voice. Perhaps he'd had a few drinks, which might account for the slight differences?

Did she want it to be Lord Ryon?

Before she could ask him, Lord Blackwell came into view. He would reach her within a minute. Lord Ryon dropped her hand unceremoniously and walked away without a backwards glance, abandoning Lucy in the middle of the sea of rushing bodies, joining another group of his friends.

Behind Lord Blackwell, Evost approached at a quick trot. Lucy pretended not to see her and hastened away before they flanked her.

Narrowly avoiding them both, her hips swished as she moved through the crowd. Careful not to draw attention, she reached the end of the hall and ducked down the stairs to the study.

Nine

Despite the throng of people going in the opposite direction, the study was bustling. Lucy wondered if everyone had the same idea of a romantic rendezvous.

The study differed from what she'd imagined. The ceiling wasn't as tall now that it was lit. Shelves reached only two stories, with sliding ladders that slid around the perimeter of the room. Thankfully, she hadn't run into one of those in the dark.

The wall sconce looked much less sharp.

This room was too formal and not the cozy, intimate place she'd pictured. She couldn't help but wonder if her imaginings of the mysterious man were also completely off.

She kept herself to the edge of the room, pretending to look into the glass-housed bookshelves and glancing quickly at the other guests.

It was impossible to know if *he* was there. She recognized Lord Dartsmooth and his wife—*he'd* said he wasn't married. Lord Greld was much too short. Three gentlemen she didn't know played cards at a table, and two ladies read near a fireplace. Lucy tried to remember the names her uncle had provided. She knew one of them was related to someone who'd inherited lands on the southern border of Rockville; but none of this mattered to her.

Trailing her finger along the ledge, she wondered if a maid would come behind her to polish everything she'd touched.

The hair prickled on the back of Lucy's neck. She took a minute to hide the alarm over someone coming up behind her, then turned.

"Jasper! I mean, Lord Terrington—" Lucy exclaimed, lowering her voice when heads swivelled in their direction. "What are you doing here?"

"I prefer people call me Jasper, and you sound disappointed. Were you expecting someone else?" he asked. Lucy was thankful she'd ruled him out the other evening—unless he could turn his accent on and off at will. She studied him again. He was the right height and had a confident air about him, but he was much too old for her, and something in the way he looked at everyone made her uncomfortable. It was as if he could see invisible clouds over everyone's heads and was hoping rain would pour down on them.

"I'm looking for a book, but alas, I can't find it."

When Jasper didn't make a move away from her, she shifted uncomfortably from one foot to the other. "Is there something else I could help you with?"

"I need to talk to you," he stated.

Lucy stared after him as he took a seat in a large black chair on the far side of the room. She joined him, having no idea what he could need to talk to her about. It couldn't be a coincidence that he asked to speak with her right after her night with the mysterious man. He hadn't said more than two words to her since Lady Cristelle left. Lucy bit the inside of her lip. The only person she wanted it to be less than Jasper was Lord Blackwell.

He pulled out a knife and started flicking it absently.

"Don't stab me," Lucy said sharply. It came out more commanding than she'd intended.

"I wasn't planning on it," he replied, confused.

"Lady Cristelle told me about an unfortunate incident with a blade and your cousin."

Lady Cristelle, a friend of Lucy's, had recently returned from being presumed dead. No one believed that the man she'd fallen in love with was Jasper's cousin—but no one dared to question Jasper. When she'd asked Lord Daye why Lady Cristelle could do whatever she liked, he'd replied that she had guild control. Freedom came with power, he'd said.

Lucy didn't believe him—everyone around her held power, and no one had the freedom to do what they liked.

Jasper closed the blade and tucked it into his jacket pocket. He sat properly, his black shirt buttoned up to his chin. Ghosts danced behind his dark eyes. He looked tense without the item to play with, and Lucy almost regretted commenting on it.

"I need your help. I'm looking for your Aunt… Lady Daye." The confession startled Lucy and made Jasper even more uncomfortable. This was not what she'd expected. He was not confessing to be the man in the dark, thank goodness. Letting out a breath, she leaned toward him, one arm on the chair.

"Why are you looking for her? Has my uncle hired you?"

"No one hired me, and I prefer you not mention this to him or anyone else. I am doing this as a friend—for her." He shifted again. For someone so sinister looking, he was dreadful at hiding a lie. He was clearly very uncomfortable with coming to her for help. How intriguing.

"How can I possibly help? I've spent most of my time avoiding Lord Blackwell, my uncle, or the woman hired to *educate* me." Lucy glanced around the room, wondering if mentioning her would summon the beast. Jasper followed her gaze around the room.

"Why are you avoiding Lord Blackwell?"

"My uncle is obsessed with me offering to marry him. Do you know him?" Lucy picked up a book off the table between them and flipped through the soft pages.

"No—but I'll look into it."

His own offer of assistance came quickly, and Lucy watched the wheels turning. Whether it was out of misguided protectiveness or because Lord Blackwell might be another part of the puzzle, she didn't know.

"Again—how can I help? I've already tried looking but found nothing. I was on Orion when she disappeared, but I didn't even know she was there until I saw her at the ball. I talked to her for only a few minutes. She said nothing to indicate she was leaving. There was a whole situation with Wynter and Helix, and then she was gone."

Lucy had been on the same planet. Her aunt had ignored her without a second thought, but she must have known what her leaving would do to Lucy. *Bitter* wasn't the right word, but it irked her.

"Give yourself a little more credit. I'm not asking what you remember. Hundreds of people saw her at the ball. I'm asking for your skills. I've heard the staff (not on Nova- Manor, of course) call you Lucy—not Lady Lucy. You make friends everywhere you go, and people will talk to you. Staff, maids, butlers. Someone has to know something."

The way he spoke about her engaging with the staff was not said in a condescending tone, but almost admiringly. Lucy snapped the book shut, her earlier suspicions aroused again. Perhaps this whole request about finding Lady Daye was a ruse to get close to her.

"Can you say the word darkness for me?" Lucy asked, testing out her theory.

"If I do, will you agree to help me?"

Lucy nodded, and he repeated the word back to her in the most boring way possible. No thrill shivered up her spine—she was safe.

Although asking for her to help find Lady Daye was like trying to grab smoke. She still doubted she could do anything—surely if someone had information, they would have come forward.

But perhaps this was the answer to her problems. She didn't plan on sticking around Valtine, and maybe finding her aunt was the best chance of going back to her own life, at least for a time. Lucy weighed her options carefully. On the one hand, Jasper was not known to be kind and had his own mystery surrounding him, even though Lady Cristelle had trusted him. On the other hand, if they found her aunt, she wouldn't have to marry Lord Blackwell. And if Jasper was willing to help her learn more about Lord Blackwell without having to talk to him, then maybe there was more than one way to get away from him.

"I don't do things halfway. If I agree to help, I'm all in.

Sneaky outfits and everything. I'm kidding… about the outfits. Goodness, you should see your face. You find out what you can about Lord Blackwell and how I might thwart Lord Daye's plans, and I'll investigate my aunt's disappearance. Tell me what you know so far."

Jasper leapt at her acceptance, and she realized he was in earnest. He leaned in, their heads close. Lucy couldn't believe the speed and intensity with which Jasper told her everything. She sat motionless as he gave an extensive list of everything he'd already done. He'd already spoken with everyone who had any connection with Lady Daye. The same story repeated over and over. Few spent time with her outside of formal events. They never saw her shopping or in town. He located the mysterious woman in charge of her gowns, but if she knew anything, she wasn't telling Jasper. Lucy wasn't surprised. Staff of any kind rarely talked to those in the court—and certainly not to someone like Jasper, despite his best efforts.

There were whispers and rumours about her uncle causing the disappearance. More than one person had heard them arguing two days before she left. After the argument, Lord Daye had been unwell for a few weeks. This was new information to Lucy. Search parties were investigating as far as the outer planets, and more than one ambassador was looking for her—but they kept it all silent, of course.

"Perhaps—together—we can figure this out," Lucy said, making a deal with the second most dark and mysterious lord she'd encountered so far on the Nova-Manor.

Ten

For the next three days, Lucy didn't have a single moment to herself. Evost woke her early each morning. Ice baths were followed by her corset, then topped with a dull gown. Lessons in a small morning room followed the ritual.

Each lecture reviewed etiquette, rules, and proper behaviour. Lucy had memorized said rules before she'd turned ten. She never had trouble knowing or remembering them. She just didn't care and told Evost as much but quickly learned that Evost already knew. The lessons were meant to be more of a slow torture than an actual education.

Lucy did her best to keep her eyes open and her back straight. Signs of slouching would give away her more comfortable corset.

After her lessons, Lucy rested in her room. She pulled out a small notebook and wrote the names of everyone she'd talked to about her aunt, and everyone she would talk to if she ever made it back to Orion.

In the afternoons, she was let loose on the gathering. Attempting to stay off Evost's radar, she was polite and careful and asked as many questions as possible about Lady Daye.

Much like Jasper's efforts, no one wanted to talk about her disappearance. It wasn't proper or pleasant. The hunt for information regarding her aunt began to consume her and carried an intense sadness she hadn't expected.

With every conversation, the lords and ladies continued to decline in her estimation of them. They made casual remarks about the balls and parties her aunt hosted, and Lucy got a clear picture of her aunt's life on Valtine. Miserable. They remembered the heavily scented songbird flowers, the dreadful dinners. Inclusion and distance at the same time.

Based on everything she learned, Lady Daye wouldn't want to return.

More than their disdain for Lady Daye, she sensed the fear they all carried; Lucy was a crack that needed repair. One strike of the hammer, and everything would crumble. They were kind and welcoming only to the extent that it would maintain their world. If it looked like Lucy might cause more problems, they all wanted to be the first to put distance between them. No amount of relaxation or fancy decorations could hide the unrest.

Her information-seeking hadn't been a complete waste of time. She'd befriended a few staff who were willing to talk to her and even got a pair of the flowing pants she'd admired the first day and a simple top to go with them—she hid the clothes under her pillow so Evost wouldn't find them. The staff had also provided updates on the whereabouts of her cat, who by all accounts was enjoying himself and was well fed, alleviating her worries. She'd seen him once, but he took off the moment Evost appeared.

By the fourth night, she needed a distraction. A butler quietly informed her that he'd seen Nix in the direction of the study on more than one occasion, and she might find him there.

Armed wearing the hidden pants and top instead of a sheet, she journeyed back to the study.

"Hello," Lucy called into the darkness, wondering why she hadn't brought her lamp with her. Feeling her way in the dark, she carefully avoided the ladders. She paused, certain she'd heard a soft purr from Nix. Lucy called to him, and he quickly found her. She picked him up and patted the top of his head.

Passing a cluster of chairs, she walked to the far wall. Searching without a lamp was much harder carrying a cat. She lowered herself toward an empty chair; then, finding no one, she moved onto the next one.

She connected with a warm body and let out a loud shriek, which caused Nix to take off again.

"Why didn't you say something? Or please tell me you aren't dead."

The laugh indicated not dead.

She flopped into the empty chair beside him.

"Do you sit here every night, brooding in the dark? Or were you hoping I'd come back?" Lucy asked, waiting for the thundering in her heart to settle.

"What if it's both? Although I feel it is an unfair game to play. I know who you are, and you have yet to figure out my identity."

"Yes, unfair to you. Because you already know that our friendship is doomed, and I get to live out the mystery of believing a hundred different possibilities."

"Is that what you want? Or are you just bored?"

"Definitely just bored. Why do you sit in the dark alone?" Lucy wondered what it would be like to sit for any length of time—alone—in the dark, not moving. She'd barely lasted ten minutes in her room without needing some form of distraction.

"I'm restless when I'm not on a planet. Somehow, my room makes that worse. I find a dark, quiet place calming."

She couldn't imagine this being comforting, but the study did provide an odd type of distraction for the mind. Lucy nestled into the high-back chair. Whoever read books here knew how to pick something that felt comforting and formidable at the same time—much like reading.

"Why did you come back to the study, if not for the quiet darkness?" The way he said darkness sent a trill up her spine— definitely not Jasper.

"Well, you see—the last time I was here, I forgot to pick up a book I'd been looking for about glass birds."

Why had she come back? If he hadn't been here, would she have stayed on her own? She pulled her feet up and crossed them, her knees resting on the large arm rests.

"I borrowed that one a week ago and lost it. I'm sorry, your search will be in vain," he said. Lucy laughed and relaxed into what she knew would be a pleasant conversation.

"Alright, for that one, you earned the truth. I came looking for my cat Nix because his company is better than anyone else's on this ship. Which sounds terrible, but I've talked to too many horrible people over the past few days. This place is slowly killing me. I want to go home to Orion. I don't care what happens to all the Daye wealth and lands—I don't. Not because lands and people aren't important, but because people better than my uncle or myself will probably take control, and I don't see that as a bad thing. I don't fit into this world, and the more I see of it, the less I want to. Except there's a mysterious stranger in the study who makes it all worth it. It really should be a paid position. Everyone deserves a mysterious friend."

Lucy let out a huge breath. She hadn't meant to say all of that, but weariness consumed her.

"Do you always say what you're thinking?"

"Oh no! I don't think words are fast enough to keep up with all the thoughts. Evost is afraid my future husband won't like my talking."

"What are you afraid of?"

"That my future husband won't like my talking—I don't plan on stopping."

He laughed again, and a weight lifted off Lucy. It was a real laugh, deep and full. Not fake, or controlled, or worse—annoyed. She hadn't heard a laugh like that since she left Josephine on Valtine. The ache of loneliness eased, and Lucy let the moment bring a small measure of comfort.

Eleven

They talked well into the night. Lucy shared about life growing up on Orion, the things she loved most about the guilds, and her joy in space travel. He shared stories of his sisters and their pleasant life on Valtine. His family had settled on the eastern shores of a smaller island. The Dayes did not have an estate there, and the way he described it made her want to visit. He told her of his dislike for space travel, but the increasing necessity for it.

The conversation took a turn when Lucy complained again about the court.

"It's not always this bad. I understand why you find it tiring, but you are in the very heart of the Valtine Court. People put up walls when they are threatened. The bigger the threat, the higher the wall."

"Are you calling me a threat? I'm wounded." Lucy put her hand to her chest dramatically, even though he couldn't see her.

"The eyes of the Valtine Court are on you. Change is coming regardless, but someone like you heralds the winds."

"Are you threatened by my freedoms?" Lucy asked, genuinely curious. Was he afraid of the coming changes?

"I suppose I'm envious. Not everyone can exercise the same level of freedom. If I mimed an alligator, they would immediately remove me from Nova-Manor. Disgrace would descend on my sisters, and my corset-adjusting days would be over."

"I was a hippopotamus. And I don't agree with you—because if everyone stopped behaving so carefully, it would all be over, and we could continue doing all the good in Valtine without the nonsense. You all don't even cry when someone dies. But I see your point because there is no one whom I need to protect, not even myself." Her words trailed off, and she wondered if she would act differently if there was someone counting on her, someone other than Lord Daye.

Silence enveloped them. After a minute, he reached across the distance and touched her elbow, giving her arm a gentle, reassuring squeeze.

The soft hum of the ship gave her a moment's peace. Then she felt awful for being so harsh.

"I'm sorry I'm so sullen, but I can't see the value in nonsensical rules. I imagine at least half of the adults would be prone to bouts of silliness if given the chance. I'm not accustomed to being dreary. Valtine is exquisite. My maid, Josephine, has had a splendid time. I've enjoyed the dresses and the parties, and I've improved my pickpocket skills." The last part escaped her lips without a thought.

His rich laughter echoed around the room, and she warmed, knowing she had caused it again.

"You don't believe me? I can do it blindfolded. Being a lady is dreadfully dull unless one applies oneself to all sorts of odd pursuits. You are not the only one with talents that can be performed in the dark." Lucy blushed, then rushed to add, "I'm talking about fixing my corset, of course."

"Show me," he said, his voice still full of merriment. The chair scraped along the floor slightly, and he stood. It was very dark. She stood as well but had to reach forward, groping in the dark until she had his hand.

"It's simple, really. Ladies are often taught to strategically, never dramatically, ever so slightly lean into their dance partners." In the dark, she sensed his height, half a head taller than she was. Not as tall as Jasper, taller than Lord Ryon. He smelled like nothing. No overwhelming hints of mint or pine that many of the men favoured. He didn't smell bad either. She almost wanted to lean in and see if his shirt at least hinted of the lavender cleaners favoured on Valtine.

Focusing on the task at hand, she bumped into him. "Oh sorry, I didn't mean to do that. I messed it all up."

He steadied her, his hand like a flame on her arm. "It's nearly pitch black in here, so I can't blame you for your failure. You'll just have to try again."

Lucy held a small pocket knife that she'd pulled from his breast pocket.

She found his other hand and held it, the cool metal pressed between their palms.

He closed her fingers one at a time over the knife. She liked the way her heart rate increased and her stomach fluttered. The air rushed out of the room.

"Please keep it as a token of my apology. I completely underestimated you. But I suggest you keep it hidden from

Evost."

They were standing so close, and Lucy knew the first time they'd met didn't compare to this. Her head was spinning with all the dramatic notions of what falling in love would feel like, and the best part was she never had to see him again.

"Do you want to kiss me?" Lucy asked, wishing all his thoughts were shared out loud like hers were.

"I'm too old for you. And there is one disadvantage—I know who you are, but you do not know who I am. Not the type of circumstances I prefer for kissing."

"Yes, I understand this is all very improper—and you're being ever the gentleman, blah blah blah… I asked if you wanted to kiss me."

Lucy held her breath, waiting in the darkness.

"I wanted to kiss you the moment you brought lambs into a ball," he said. Lucy felt his breath on her cheek and realized he had leaned in much closer than she had expected. Was he about to break his own rule and kiss her, despite his better judgement? Lucy held her breath and closed her eyes, waiting for him to close the last of the small distance between them, ready to feel his lips on hers.

But the kiss never came; he pulled away abruptly as light streamed in through the door.

"Lucy!" Evost's shrill voice called from the open door. It pierced through the darkness like a crazed bat.

Lucy's face flamed. How had that dreadful woman found her?

"I'm here—not doing anything I shouldn't be. I'm coming, I just couldn't sleep. No need to worry." Annoyed and frustrated, Lucy darted away from the mysterious man. If he was caught with her, a scandal would reflect poorly on his sisters. She tucked the knife into the pocket of the pants she shouldn't be wearing and hoped Evost wouldn't notice her attire, but didn't count on it.

"You'd have me believe you were sitting alone in the dark doing nothing?" Evost snapped.

Lucy made her way carefully to the stream of light. Forgetting the tall ladders, she bumped into one, sending a slight pain through her elbow.

"My own rooms are too small—I'm a lady accustomed to a substantial amount of space," Lucy ground out, hoping to reach the door before Evost flooded the whole room with light. "And to be honest, it's lovely being around books. I feel like I'm absorbing the information. I heard it works better in the dark because then you can't be distracted by all the fantastic spines. I want to be mature and wise and not so silly, and this felt like the right place to contemplate all of those things."

Lucy prattled on. The light from the door illuminated most of the room as Evost opened it the rest of the way. Lucy quickly followed, not looking back.

Evost led Lucy back to her rooms, like another stray lamb returning to its pen.

"I have never failed at producing a lady of fine quality," she said. It sounded like a pledge to herself more than to Lucy.

"Which means everything you do is a failure," Lucy muttered under her breath, irritated that Evost had interrupted what might have been the most romantic kiss of her life.

Twelve

Lucy was being punished for her late night out—and for the pants. The ladies' breakfast room smelled like rich coffee and cocoa. Fresh berries and oranges decorated the table. But in front of her sat a bowl of bland yogurt and a small dish of dried fruit.

None of the women dared to look at her.

Lucy wanted to stand and scream, for even polite conversation was no longer allowed.

The ladies' breakfast room was one place where the ladies could let their guard down, which made it even more painful to see them acting perfectly. They all knew that any slip-up might be talked about afterwards.

It infuriated her that Evost, a woman without title, commanded so much control. With so little effort, she cowed the wills of an entire room of well-born, intelligent women.

Lucy balanced her spoon on the edge of her bowl and thumped a fist down on it, sending a spray of dried fruit into the air. Then she stood, her chair scraping loudly across the floor as she left.

She hoped someone would tell Evost all about it.

* * *

Nothing changed over the next two days. The lectures were exceptionally long, and her food rations decreased. In the middle of the night, Lucy tried to leave her room, but a butler stood guard at the end of the hall, making escape impossible.

She wondered if the mysterious man in the study waited for her. But sadly, she reminded herself that he knew who she was. If he'd wanted to talk to her, he would have found her.

During her garden walks and dining, she inspected every man who passed. Too tall, too short. Perhaps her mysterious man was the tallish gentleman looking into a pond of fish, but she couldn't remember his name, and he didn't even look her way.

Drinking her tea on the third morning, she was planning an escape for later that night, pondering how to sneak past her guard. The early stages of a plan had just formed when a ripple of news rose like a wave and crashed over the guests. It swam from one lady, to a nearby attendant, to the maid who watered the plants.

A final ball would take place in two days, after which the Nova-Manor would be closing. As quickly as the mysterious mansion had appeared, it would depart. What this meant for her, she didn't know. Lord Daye had been absent for most of her time on the Nova-Manor, and there had been no communication about what would happen next.

She'd learned little to help Jasper, and he, in turn, had barely spoken to her again. What had been a promising partnership had quickly worn thin.

Her search for the mysterious man was replaced with the pressing need to find Nix. She hoped to locate him on her own, but she might need the help of the staff. He could be quite sneaky when he wanted to be.

The search began in a tropical sitting area, but it was quickly abandoned when she spied Lord Daye nearby speaking with Lord Blackwell. Their heads were bowed close together, as if they shared a great secret. Lucy avoided contact and hustled toward the gardens, then ducked behind a hedge.

She had wandered the maze a few times already. It wasn't difficult, but it did afford couples or conspirators a few corners in which to speak privately. In several places, tall bridges covered in moss and flowers rose over the hedges, crossing blocked paths and making the hiding places obsolete.

A soft meow echoed from above her. Lucy quickly ascended the mossy stairs. Nix lay sprawled out, his orange fur fluffing out over the green leaves. He glanced at her lazily, licked his paw, then rubbed his head on the hedge. He clearly wasn't hungry or concerned that he'd been on his own for the past number of days.

She considered crawling out to reach him until voices from below caught her attention. Not wanting to intrude on a private moment, she shrank back from the edge. Lucy immediately recognized the couple. Peeking below the bridge, she spied Lord Ryon stepping toward Lady Zandra.

Her wide-brimmed lace hat blocked her from view. It was a wonder Lord Ryon could make advances considering the volume of that hat. Pink, purple, and crimson flowers dashed in all directions out of the confection. She took a moment to consider whether she was jealous, then shook off the notion when Zandra's voice rose above their quiet conversation. She put a hand up to stop Lord Ryon, which he promptly ignored.

It was much too early for Ryon to be drinking haze—and he had no excuse, as Zandra clearly wasn't interested. Lucy gave the girl a moment to handle the situation without embarrassment, but when the plea turned to a fearful cry, Lucy knew she had to intervene.

She looked for a quick way down, but the path from the bridge wound around in a long arc, and she couldn't follow it without getting turned around. Lucy hiked up her skirts, wishing for the confiscated flowy pants, and swung one leg then the other over the railing.

Vines snapped and crackled as she half slid, half clawed her way to the ground. Her dress picked up a line of green foliage and stains. The branches scraped her arms, and the landing sent a jolt through her legs. She lost her balance, fell backwards, and caught herself scraping her hands on the stone path.

Lord Ryon immediately stepped back from Zandra, anger and fear flashing across his face.

"Oh, I'm so sorry!" Lucy exclaimed. "I reached for my cat and must have fallen." As if on cue, Nix let out a loud purr and swung his tail over the edge of the opposite side.

Unshed tears threatened to fall from Zandra's eyes.

Anger roiled in Lucy's chest. She wanted to kick Lord Ryon, but her ankle exploded with pain when she tried to stand on it, and she tumbled back onto her bottom. Zandra stood frozen in place.

Lord Ryon swaggered over to Lucy. His confidence made

her wonder again if he was the mysterious man from the library. Her face flamed, remembering some of the things she'd told him. If it was Ryon, he didn't deserve her secrets. He rolled his shoulders and grinned with his teeth.

"I'm so sorry to ruin your time together, but why don't you run ahead and let them know I might need some ice for this?" Lucy said pointedly to Zandra.

The young woman pushed past them both. Lucy wasn't sure if she headed in the right direction or not, but at least she was away from Lord Ryon.

He gallantly helped her to her feet, brushing a leaf from her shoulder. Then he cleared debris from her gown. She swatted him away roughly, showing more force than Zandra had.

"My gown is utterly ruined. There's no point in trying to save it," she said. Testing her ankle, she found that standing sent a shot of pain up and around it as soon as she put weight down.

"Who said anything about saving the dress?" he said and winked at Lucy.

This time, she did not blush but puffed out her cheeks as if she were going to throw up.

"You need a gentleman's help in order to walk," he said and gallantly bowed, offering his arm to her.

"You are far from a gentleman," Lucy spat back, staring at the offered arm.

He brought his other arm to his chest in feigned hurt. "And here I thought you to be a rule breaker."

"Some things are rules, and some things are just wrong."

He ignored her and offered his arm again with a wink; she knew she had to take it in order to get back out through the maze.

If Lord Ryon was annoyed with her intervention, he didn't show it. He chatted with her and carefully cleared the path as she walked beside him. The picture of a perfect lord of Valtine. Lucy wanted to throw up in earnest.

They quickly found the exit. It was unfortunately a popular location, and a crowd gathered before Lucy could sneak away.

She wondered how terrible she looked and found it impossible to hold herself up straight the way a corset should. Her ruse was at an end if Evost laid an eye on her.

"Hello, uncle," Lucy squawked, spying him from across the low gardens. She glanced back at the maze, noting the unfortunate timing of Zandra's exit.

"You should have seen it, uncle," Lucy said loudly, drawing attention away from Zandra. She stepped away from the maze, giving the girl time to get away. "I told Lord Ryon that I could climb up to the bridge. Those vines look so sturdy—you'd think they'd hold my weight. He tried to stop me, of course, but once I set my mind on something… " Lucy waved her hand absently in the air.

Lord Daye's face went red, but he couldn't reprimand her with so many others watching. Clearly not wanting to stick around for another lecture, Lord Ryon offered a dazzling, thankful smile before detangling himself from her arm. He bowed, and the entire crowd saw him wink at her. Their imaginations were left free to fill in the blanks.

Lucy held her breath. Her ankle was screaming, and she needed to get back to her rooms, but Lord Ryon had fled the scene, abandoning her.

Gingerly putting pressure on her foot for even a second

caused pain to shoot up from her heel. Her balance faltered. She reached for the nearest tree, but it was at least two steps away, and she feared she'd fall again.

Lord Blackwell stepped in to assist her.

The crowd was silently growing, watching and waiting.

It certainly wasn't the introduction Lord Daye had hoped for, but there was no way to avoid it now.

"Lady Lucy, I would like to introduce you to Lord Blackwell."

Lord Blackwell looked embarrassed, and she almost felt bad for him. It wasn't his fault Lord Daye had decided on the match. He wore a casual shirt, with the sleeves rolled up and showing his large forearms. Morning stubble hadn't been shaved, but his hair was perfectly set. He looked very much a dangerously boring lord if ever she saw one.

Lord Blackwell would certainly want nothing to do with her now. He wasn't even looking down at her but was focused on where Lord Ryon had fled. He placed an arm around her waist to help hold her weight. An audible sigh echoed from the ladies around her, and the air lifted.

Stability.

Lord Blackwell was the stability they were all hoping would lead the richest family on Valtine.

Thankfully, they were not to be gawked at for long, for Lord Blackwell silently led her away from the swooning crowd.

Thirteen

Trees stretched over Lucy and Lord Blackwell like silent guards in the breezeless oasis. Birds fluttered and chirped. Lucy wondered if they knew they were in a cage and not flying free.

A thorn found its way into the side of her shoe. It stuck in her heel adding to the sting from all the little scrapes and cuts she'd accumulated. Lord Blackwell said no more than a few mumbled apologies when his speed didn't match hers.

Her arm burned where he held her up, but it relieved the pressure on her ankle. Dizzy from the awkward half hobble, she stumbled as they neared the entrance to the manor.

Lord Blackwell stopped and moved as if he would lift her.

"No. I'd rather walk, thank you."

He waved off the staff, who rushed toward them, and continued to lead her in blessed silence down the halls.

She redirected him toward the wing where Evost had been housing her. When they reached the sign pointing to the study, she hesitated, then led him toward her room.

He frowned again.

She glanced behind, wishing instead to hide in the study's comfort—to curl up in one of the large chairs and let her pain leak into the books. A leaf from her gown fluttered to the floor.

A deep dread settled over her when they reached her room.

Evost appeared like an unwelcome ghost. Lucy wanted to suggest she had a future career as a magician, but the commander immediately started barking orders.

"Thank you, Lord Blackwell. I'll take it from here."

He hesitated, as if he didn't want to let her go, then bowed and left without another word.

Lucy's cheeks flamed with embarrassment. What a simply boring man. At least she had provided an excuse for him to refuse her.

Everything ached, her stomach growled, and Nix was still missing. What a dreadful way to end her time on the Nova-Manor.

The lady's maids were efficient but careful. The dress was difficult to remove without making her wince.

Lucy braced herself for the cold plunge, but the water steamed gloriously for a change. Oils scented with jasmine made the water glide like silk over each cut. Like a bee sting, they burned, then eased. Lucy sunk in until the heat tickled the back of her neck.

Evost gathered her clothing, including the corset, and left the room just as wordlessly as Blackwell had.

As soon as she left, the maids expressed their concern. According to one of the maids, a gardener had seen what had really happened with Lady Zandra, but was afraid to speak up for Zandra's sake. Lucy wondered if it wouldn't be better for the next young lady in Lord Ryon's path if the truth was known, but Zandra was new to the court, and Lucy was already on the fringe. She doubted anyone would believe her. The staff told her how brave she had been and assured her someone was already trying to find Nix.

Once out of the bath, she was wrapped in a fluffy robe. They brushed her hair until it shimmered down her back. Purple flowing pants and a sleeveless shirt sat on top of a pile of warm towels.

None of this made sense—something had caused a change in Evost, and Lucy dearly wanted to know what.

Once she was dressed, a medic arrived and wrapped her ankle.

"Evost says you are to rest this evening," one maid said.

Lucy thanked her. Tears brightened the young girl's eyes, and Lucy gave her a swift hug, then retired to her room. Despite the early afternoon hour, she fell into a deep sleep.

She awoke to a soft knock on her door and opened it to find a food cart. Apparently, rest for the evening meant she had to stay in for dinner. She brought it inside, ate the warm pie before the rest, then lay back in her bed.

The familiar boredom set in. After such a long nap earlier, this silence made her restless. When it reached midnight, she slipped from her room. There was no guard at the end of the hall.

Perhaps Evost didn't expect her to venture out with a sore ankle.

This time with a bright lantern, she limped down the hall to the study.

Checking every chair, she was disappointed to find it empty.

Turning the lantern off, she sat in the dark room. She made a few loud noises that echoed and died.

Silence was hard. It was peaceful and large. And lonely.

It made her think about the past few days and after only a few moments of contemplation, she knew she no longer wanted him to be a mystery.

Finding one of the longer sofas, she stretched out and waited. She wanted to see him with the lights on, needed to find out who he really was and say a proper goodbye. She thought they'd be at the Nova-Manor for weeks, and she'd have time.

She had no idea how much time had passed when she awoke, but she remained alone.

* * *

The following days were a flurry of activity as the Nova-Manor readied for the last ball and the immediate departure. Her ankle still ached but had already decreased in swelling and would be fine within a few days.

Evost did not corset her for the evening and draped her in a deep blue gown. This ball was not for dancing but for making plans. To find out who was going where and when. For everyone to make sure they weren't left out. The dress was still beyond simple, but at least the rich fabric was perfectly fitted and flattering. A single sapphire hung around her neck, suspended on a sparkling silver chain.

She was a picture of grace and elegance as she balanced a plate of sweets in one hand and a glass of fizzing champagne in the other. She lifted the plate up to her mouth to take a bite of the soft cake balancing on the edge. Lord Daye swiftly took her champagne, freeing her hand. Lucy decided not to push her luck and brought the plate back down to a reasonable height.

Lord Daye stood beside her in a matching navy suit. His lip curled up at the edge in a half smile.

"We depart in the morning with the other guests."

"Where are we going this time? I really need some time to rest my ankle."

"We depart for Orion on the Aurora."

Lucy gasped and almost dropped her plate. A deep and unexpected joy bubbled within her and threatened to burst from her eyes in a torrent of relief.

"Compose yourself. This changes nothing. The only reason I am allowing this is because your Lord Blackwell has assured me there is an understanding between you. There is a meeting about a summit on Orion, which makes it natural we should go. His business also takes him to Orion, and we travel as a company."

Her moment of excitement deflated into a confused muddle. Lord Blackwell had not said more than two words to her. If this was an attempt to save her reputation after the garden, she would need to set it straight. Helping her to her room did not constitute an understanding.

Lord Daye grabbed her arm and squeezed it tightly, all the while remaining a picture of calm for the crowd. "If you have not declared it publicly by the midway station, I will have you brought back to Valtine. So if this is a ruse—you will not get away with it."

"Kindly release my arm, or I swear I will yell 'potato' as loudly as I can," Lucy threatened. She swallowed a lump, the cakes now too sweet and the bubbles turning in her stomach. The ridiculous threat granted her freedom from her uncle's grasp, and he handed back her champagne.

"You have mere weeks until the midway," Lord Daye said, then nodded to a passing lord who did not slow to speak with them.

Lucy patted his hand reassuringly, and desperate for a moment alone, walked away. Gliding past the kaleidoscope of twirling dancers, she retreated to the far side of the grand hall to hide and collect her thoughts.

She was heading to Orion—home—but on the condition she marry Blackwell.

Jasper found her hiding from the guests. She smiled weakly at him and waited for the flutter of fear to settle before filling him in on her plight.

"I heard you climbed a garden wall to impress Lord Ryon and now Lord Daye is anxious to leave the Nova-Manor." Jasper stated, filling her in on the current gossip.

"I was trying to hide from Lord Blackwell, not impress Lord Ryon. What utter nonsense, and it didn't work anyway, and now Lord Blackwell and I *have an understanding*. Did you learn anything about him?" Lucy asked earnestly.

"Nothing. Which means there has to be something. His family is above reproach. There isn't a single mark on the family's Idex. They appear to be genteel, intelligent, and kind folk. No one knows why Lord Blackwell has never married; all of his sisters have. He is as eligible as it gets, although with all of his sisters, finances could be an issue. I know these types— they're hiding something. And you? What have you found?"

"Little as well. Lady Daye was unfortunately not well-liked

but reasonably feared. Maybe she just ran away. Unless you can give me a reason why you think she didn't, which, by the look you are giving me, you aren't going to do. As you know, we are headed to Orion—finally—and perhaps I'll be able to learn more there. Will you be joining us on the Aurora?"

Jasper nodded. At least something was working in her favour. Lucy pulled Jasper's arm and turned him in the other direction, avoiding the incoming Lord Blackwell. It had all been too much at once, and she did not want to talk to the man until she'd formed a plan.

Home to Orion… and a marriage proposal. Like sour pudding wrapped in sweet bread. It was freedom and a trap wrapped up into one.

Fourteen

Lucy went directly from the Nova-Manor to the Aurora without returning to Valtine. She didn't mind not being able to say goodbye in person. The unrest of the Valtine Court followed them onto the Aurora as a horde of ladies and lords, more than usual, filled the ship. Rumblings of a summit being held on Orion had swayed many who otherwise would have stayed behind on Valtine.

Twice the size of the Obsidian, the grand luxury cargo ship's fifteen floors wound around a circular core. At the centre of each floor was either a dining room, lounge area, pool deck, or other entertaining room.

The Aurora's captain naturally put Lucy in a lady's suite, alongside the other young women. Unlike the Nova-Manor, there were some things here Evost could not influence. Large baths and pools, a private breakfast room, and every imaginable spa amenity ensured the traveller's comfort on the long voyage. As they were returning to Orion, Josephine was summoned from Valtine and joined her lady on the ship. The captain made a specific request that Nix was to be kept in her maid's rooms. Lucy wanted to protest, but he kindly acknowledged the pet and understood her desire to have it with her, softening her to his request. And after losing Nix on the Nova-Manor, perhaps it was for the best.

Lucy wasted no time telling Josephine about all that had happened, especially regarding the corset Evost made her wear, which had not returned since the garden. Josephine cheered triumphantly and then wept when Lucy informed her they had not broken free from Evost. The stubborn woman had settled into a maid's room one floor below but assured Lucy she would never be far away. Lucy was determined to not let it get her down. She was on her way home.

The pretty ship provided comforts Valtine never could. Lucy took time to enjoy a full recovery from her injured ankle. She spent days in the luxury of the spas, and a bit too much time dreaming about the man in the dark library whom she'd never said farewell to.

Lord Daye, however, was not faring so well. He despised space travel and rarely left Valtine. The medic had been called to his room three times in less than a day. Lucy almost felt pity for him, but without his control, she had more freedom.

"We've spent weeks on the ladies' floor," Josephine said, breaking Lucy's concentration as she stacked little cards on top of each other.

The maid held up a peach confection that floated with puffs of tulle and blue peacock feathers. It was billowy and over-the-top. There was no way Evost had approved the gown.

Lucy squealed and took the dress from Josephine, spinning in place. "Where did you get that?"

"It doesn't matter where I got it. But perhaps it's time you answered Lord Blackwell and had a meeting." Josephine busied herself rearranging the little bottles on Lucy's desk, avoiding Lucy's gaze.

Lucy scowled at the dress, seeing it as a bribe to get her off the ladies' floors. She had been hiding but it was the most lovely time and she wasn't ready for it to end.

Lord Blackwell had sent multiple requests for dinner or lunch or any type of meeting, which she had ignored. She had been delaying the inevitable. But with little time until they reached the midway station, she needed to act before Evost gathered her forces, or her uncle returned her to Valtine.

Josephine helped her into the evening gown and curled her hair. "You should be grateful. He got us off Valtine, which is more than we've been able to do."

"What am I going to say to him? Thank you for helping me that one time, but I don't want to marry you? And then what? Lord Daye takes me back to Valtine?"

"I'm sure you'll think of something clever—you always do." Josephine finished the last curl and let it bob by her ear. "And I talked to a footman: Lord Blackwell is in the fourth floor lounge with the other guests from Valtine. No more delay."

"No more delay," Lucy mimicked back, then studied herself in the mirror. It felt good to feel like herself again. She would confront Lord Blackwell regarding the mysterious arrangement that had purchased her trip home.

Lucy left Josephine to clean up the mess and wound her way through the crowded halls and up the lift toward the lounge.

Soft music floated from the white grand piano, and subdued voices welcomed her. Tall red chairs with padded backs surrounded high round tables. Vases with orange and red flowers decorated the precariously thin pedestals hosting drinks and cakes all over the room. A full buffet ran across the side wall, and amber lights made the room glow.

Lucy knew she was meant to be looking for Blackwell, but spotting Jasper first, she joined him in front of an enormous fireplace. Blue and orange flames flickered behind a glass wall that reached to the ceiling.

Jasper wore all black. The flames behind him gave him a distinct devilish tinge. He looked at her as though he had something he wanted to tell her, and she let him speak first.

"I uncovered something you might want to know about your Lord Blackwell. It's not much to go on, but I knew there was something too perfect about the family. His grandfather owned and operated a security company on Corva. They are experts in Idex tracking. It's said they designed half the systems used on ships."

"I don't see why guild work would be a secret. Lady Cristelle's father owned the Inkton perfumery before passing it on to her. Guild employment might be frowned upon, but it's not entirely scandalous. Do you think Lord Daye hired him to find my aunt?"

Jasper looked down at her, condescension fixed in his gaze. "I don't think Lord Daye knows. I found out through unusual channels. As I said, not common knowledge, even in these circles. And there's a big difference between making perfumes and dealing in security. Also…"

Before he could say anything else, Lord Blackwell himself descended on them. He was dressed casually for the evening and looked unfortunately handsome.

He bowed slightly and held out a hand to Jasper. "I don't

believe I've had the pleasure," he said.

Jasper shook his hand briefly and introduced himself. Within seconds, a small blade appeared between Jasper's fingers, and he flicked it lightly open and closed. Lord Blackwell ignored the faint click, click, click and turned to Lucy.

Lucy wondered what Jasper would say if she pulled out her own knife and played with it. She'd taken to carrying the stolen blade around with her and had been practising when she remembered to. While Jasper might be amused, Lord Blackwell would certainly think it improper. She frowned at him out of imaginary spite.

"Your uncle and Evost are both watching," he nodded to a corner where they sat with fixed attention on her. "It would help if you didn't look so miserable talking to me—and you could pretend we at least know each other."

They were the first words he'd ever spoken to her. Smooth and low and completely in control. And very familiar.

"I'm not miserable," she replied cautiously.

The way he looked down at her differed greatly from the way Jasper had. As if he could see right through her.

It had been weeks. Perhaps it was her imagination, hearing what she wanted to hear—not that she wanted the mysterious man from the study to be Lord Blackwell. Oh, how utterly unfair it would be if he were. Lucy scowled, then remembered his earlier warning about the hawk-eyes trained on her and smiled with her teeth.

It couldn't be him; she wouldn't let it be him.

"Do you often travel to Orion?" Jasper asked casually, trying to smooth the moment. He looked between Lucy and Lord Blackwell, then to where Lord Daye was standing.

She had more questions for Jasper and did not want to discuss Lord Blackwell's ridiculous claim of an understanding in front of him, but she didn't know how to tell either man to leave, especially now that they had started a dull conversation about the outer planets.

Unfortunately, she was momentarily distracted. Out of the corner of her eye, she saw Lord Ryon stalking yet another young lady. The poor young woman brushed him off twice. With every step she took to the side, he took two and got closer.

Lucy tried to ignore it, but the lady looked around the room and caught her eye before opening a side door that Lucy knew led to a servant's hallway. Surely someone on the other side of the room would stop him. But no one did. Ryon was quick on her heels and looked far too pleased with himself. A deep rage boiled in Lucy's chest—how had she ever entertained caring for this man?

Without a second thought, Lucy picked a small round cupcake from the tower of treats to her left and lobbed it across the room at Lord Ryon. The frosted cannonball sailed in a high arc with extraordinary speed. A shower of sprinkles rained down on the heads of those in its flight path.

The dough hit its mark—on the closed door after Ryon had stepped through it, giving him a clean getaway. The cake stuck for a moment, then slid down to the floor, leaving a trail of thick decadent icing.

Fifteen

Silence, followed by a slow murmur, burned around the edges of the room.

"Won't you excuse me?" Lucy said politely to Jasper and Lord Blackwell. She curtsied, then followed the path of the cupcake past the stunned guests and down the narrow hallway.

She rushed breathlessly past a server carrying a tray of drinks and glimpsed Ryon entering a room at the end of the hall. Trying to stop the hammering in her chest, she sprinted toward the closing door, fueled by rage. She knew she should have said something after the garden, but Zandra's reputation was on the line. She kicked herself for following the rules instead of doing what she knew was right. There were a dozen stories she could have come up with, leaving Zandra out of it. A plan was always close at hand, yet she'd given into daydreaming about a mysterious man in the library. A man she was nearly convinced was the most dreadfully dull man she'd ever met.

Lucy stormed in after Ryon. The enormous pantry smelled

like dried fruit and flour. Rows of packaged goods and containers lined the walls. Ryon was alone, the girl nowhere in sight. Relief for the escapee mingled with fear for herself as he latched onto her arm and pulled her close.

She wished she were Lady Cristelle, who was an expert at delivering a decent punch. Cristelle had tried to teach her, and they'd practised a dozen moves, but Lucy had never quite got the hang of it, especially when wearing an overly fluffed dress.

"If you wanted to be alone with me, you could have just asked. I see you following me everywhere. I think this is what you were actually looking for." He kissed her neck, pressing his nose against her, breathing hot air into her ear. She wiggled and pushed against him with all of her strength, but he had her in a vice grip.

She didn't want this; she didn't want his sloppy mouth on her skin.

She tried to scream, but a hand pressed over her mouth.

With her left hand, she lifted the pile of tulle and kicked him in the shin.

Startled, he let go for a moment. Lucy pulled out the blade she kept in her pocket and flicked it open, trying to spin it the way she'd seen Jasper do a thousand times… it couldn't be too hard. The blade nicked the inside of his arm but then spun wildly. It tumbled back, sliced her own glove, and cut her palm when she tried to grab it. She yelped, and it clattered to the floor. Well, there was that.

Enraged, he grabbed her wrists hard enough to leave a bruise. Lucy winced. But before she could blink, she felt him being dragged away from her. His fingers scraped her arms in an attempt to hold on.

Jasper was there in a flash, and behind him stood Lord Blackwell.

Like lightning, a blade pressed against Ryon's neck, and he stopped moving. Jasper's eyes darkened as he fought for control. Lucy held her breath, hands clasped together.

"Jasper, careful," Lord Blackwell said, his voice calm and commanding. Jasper looked murderous, and Lucy feared he would actually harm Ryon—although she wasn't sure she even cared. Lord Blackwell placed a hand gently on Jasper's arm. The spell broke, and he loosened his grip, lowering the blade.

"Gentlemen," Lord Ryon said. He sniffed at Lucy and straightened his coat. "No need for the fuss. I wasn't going to hurt the lady. Just ask her. She wanted to be here with me. It was just a kiss and—" he couldn't finish his sentence as Lord Blackwell supplied a quick jab to his face.

Lucy screamed, and Lord Ryon's unconscious body crumpled to the floor.

Jasper grinned, then picked up Lucy's discarded knife, inspected it for a moment, and held it out to Lord Blackwell.

Lucy stopped breathing.

"It's not mine," Blackwell said hastily.

Jasper raised a confused brow. "It's your family crest on the side."

Lucy held out her hand, and Jasper slowly released the blade to her keeping.

"I stole it," Lucy said. Emotions roiled through her and her mind spun, trying to make all of the information fit together as she tucked the blade into her skirt pocket. Blackwell was a friend of her uncle's—they spent time together drinking tea and talking about whatever boring things they talked about.

But she'd known it the moment he spoke—and now, the way he looked at his knife and the way he looked at her confirmed, he was the mysterious man from the study.

"Perhaps someone should teach you to use it," Jasper replied, looking from Lucy to Lord Blackwell. His brows drew together, and he pulled the cuff of his sleeve.

"I offered to turn the lights on," Lord Blackwell said, ignoring Jasper.

"You handled my corset expertly, without a light," Lucy shouted back. Lucy stared at the man in front of her. She tried to picture him as the mysterious man in the shadows, but somehow she'd pictured that person as anyone but Lord Blackwell. Worse, he'd taken her corset off, and she'd been dreaming about him ever since. Her face flamed, and a spatter of blood dripped from the cut in her palm.

"I didn't know who you were at first, although it didn't take long," he stammered and reached for her hand, but she pulled back and hid it behind her.

"Why does Lord Daye think we have an understanding?" Lucy squeezed her fist, hoping to stop the blood. "Did you think our time together meant I would be okay with marrying a Valtine lord?"

"Of course not—but it was—" Blackwell started, then stopped when Lord Ryon stirred and let out a loud moan.

"I think I should go. I'll notify the captain and the medic," Jasper offered. He shifted uncomfortably and poked Lord Ryon with the toe of his shoe.

No one moved.

Lucy looked at Lord Blackwell for another minute.

He stood in silence, waiting for her to do something, to say something.

Her heart constricted more than she wanted it to. She closed her eyes, trying to think of all the things he'd said to her, all the things she'd said in return. Was this his plan? Something he'd formed with Lord Daye to trap her into marriage? Embarrassment brought a flame to her cheeks, and she recalled asking him to kiss her.

She wished she could take those words back—take all of it back.

The way Lord Blackwell had declined kissing her in the dark tipped her heart over. He could have taken advantage of the situation and used it to pressure her for marriage, but he hadn't. He was honorable and that made everything worse.

Confusion and dread filled her.

Another drop of blood fell from her palm and splattered on the floor behind her. She knew she had no one to blame but herself. If she'd never brought the lambs into the ball, she would have met him that night, politely declined to offer for marriage, and none of this would have happened.

Now she was standing face-to-face with the man she'd been dreaming about and dreading at the same time.

"I can't do this," she said.

Lucy stuffed the bloodied knife into her pocket and fled.

Sixteen

Jasper chased after her, catching up with her down the hallway. She stopped when he called and then turned to face him.

"Is there something you need to tell me about Lord Blackwell?" Jasper asked. He pulled a soft blue handkerchief from his breast pocket, the same blue as the trim on his shoes, and unfolded it. He held his hand out, and she put hers in his, palm up as he inspected the cut. It had mostly dried but stung when he pressed a bit of cloth to it.

"I'm so embarrassed. And no, he didn't hurt me or anything. I can't believe I asked him to kiss me. I didn't even know who he was and he—well, no, nothing I want to tell you about," she said, stopping herself and trying not to blush. "But you were going to tell me something else about him earlier, and I'd like to know what it was."

Indecision flickered for a moment in his eyes. He curled her fingers closed, holding the cloth tight. "Three months before Lady Daye disappeared, a butler saw her talking to Lord Blackwell. They were alone in the garden at night. He overheard nothing, but it was definitely them.”

It might be meaningless—people talked all the time—but it was an odd coincidence.“My aunt was always something of a matchmaker—perhaps my marriage to Lord Blackwell was her idea, and this is all Lord Daye’s misguided attempt at dealing with her loss.” Lucy didn’t believe her uncle was operating out of kindness, but she couldn’t rule it out. Not everything had to be secret and sinister.

But Lord Blackwell knowing Lady Daye changed things. If she’d only talked to him sooner, she could have asked him. Again, it was her fault for being bored and playing games in the darkness instead of just talking to the man.

“I’ll take care of Lord Ryon—will you be okay?” Jasper asked. He glanced back down the hall.

Lucy took a deep breath in and squared her shoulders, thankful it was Jasper who had followed her and a little sad Lord Blackwell hadn’t. “Of course I’ll be fine. I’ve done worse than throw a cupcake. I only need a bit of time to myself. Can you say something clever to Lord Blackwell that will make it not so embarrassing the next time I see him? Nevermind—just tell him I’m fine but need a bit of time. Oh, that sounds even worse. Come up with something for me, will you? And you should know, Lord Blackwell has sisters to protect. It’s best if he’s left out of the story with Lord Ryon.”

Jasper raised a brow, nodded and headed back to where Ryon was being detained.

Lucy wandered the halls, not knowing where she should go.

Everyone gave her a wide berth. The gentlemen she passed looked through her as if she didn’t exist, and the ladies pulled their skirts close to give her more room, as if touching her would somehow infect them with silliness.

The rumour of the evening spread as Lucy headed back to her rooms. The partially fabricated news overlooked Lucy's cupcake toss and focused on the black eye Ryon had received from Lord Terrington. Lord Blackwell wasn't even mentioned in the story.

As Lucy rounded the corner to her hallway, she noticed her door open and Evost standing in the way. Lucy pushed past her. If there was one person she had no patience for at the moment, it was Evost.

Evost held up her old corset, the one Lord Blackwell had adjusted.

Lucy shuddered. She'd gotten used to being without it, even with its ability to expand. But even if she put that thing back on, nothing would change. There was no way she could make an offer of marriage to Lord Blackwell now.

"Someone has tampered with this." Evost shook it violently, and Lucy rolled her eyes. "I didn't want to do this, but it appears you have learned nothing from our lessons."

"Nor am I going to!" Lucy shouted, her voice filling the room. She did not want to be reminded of the adjusted corset —of the man who'd helped her in the dark and then rescued her from Ryon.

"I've done this a hundred times and have yet to lose. I always win, and you will accept your role in this world. You are a simple, stupid girl in control of too much for her own good."

"Yes, I've been trying to tell my uncle the same thing. And what's worse, everyone else. Do you know how horribly they reacted to lambs at a ball? They were harmless balls of fluff that provided a mild annoyance, and you'd think I'd murdered someone. And yet men like Lord Ryon are excused. You are all pathetic. Everyone in the Valtine Court, everyone who goes along with anything they consider proper."

"The faster you accept your fate, the faster we can be done with all of this. With only a week until the midway, you will see reason and make a proper offer to Lord Blackwell. Lord Daye thought giving you a bit of comfort would sway you, but after today's debacle, I see it is not the case."

"It will take more than a corset to make me marry him."

"The corset would have worn you down if it hadn't been tampered with. The previous help has all been fired for not noticing. You should consider how your actions shape the course of everyone else's lives."

Lucy glared and made a mental note to find out who each of them was and ensure they were reemployed at one of her properties.

Evost snapped her fingers, and an army of maids came into the room. Fighting, Lucy struggled against them. Evost wore a sneer as Lucy's arms were held out and the lovely gown Josephine had procured was cut off. The new corset was a fine black net. It lacked boning or regular corset structure. A hum of technology filled the room as it seamlessly bound to itself and adhered to her bare skin like scales.

"I wasn't sure if it would be ready on time, but your attempts to thwart me have sped production. I will make sure you see reason. You will not speak or eat until you are ready to present yourself as the self-composed lady who will inherit the largest land titles in hex-system history."

"And what if I don't break?" Lucy asked.

Evost ignored her question. "In seven days, we will reach the midway, and you will attend the ball, where you will declare Lord Blackwell as your future husband—who, I assure you, is in complete agreement with this re-education. Everyone will see you as a perfect couple. If you don't, we will return to Valtine, and you will wear this corset for the rest of your life."

Lucy filled her lungs to scream, but like a dandelion blowing in the wind, tiny sharp pains fluttered up and down her spine and stole her voice.

Seventeen

The black netted corset adhered to her skin without any give. She tried everything she could find, but any attempt to pull, poke, or lift the fabric caused a ripple of electricity followed by a shock of pain. If she was perfectly still, the pain subsided.

Trying the door, she found it locked. There was no Josephine, no Nix, and there were no messages from Lord Blackwell either. She couldn't imagine, didn't want to imagine, what he thought of her, yet at the same time she wished he would appear, demanding to speak to her and then rescuing her from Evost.

Except that she'd told Jasper to tell Lord Blackwell she was fine. He wouldn't be looking for her.

Only when exhaustion claimed her did she sleep. Even then, she dreamed of running through fields of thorns and swimming in a lake of glass.

Days passed, and Lucy lost hope quicker than she ever would have imagined. Evost did not allow her to leave her rooms, and maids were limited and always accompanied by a footman who delivered meagre food, barely enough to keep her functioning. It would have been humiliating if she wasn't so angry. She tried screaming, tried banging on her bed. No one could hear her, or if they did, they hadn't come to help. She was quietly suffocating down the hall from a thousand other passengers.

As exhaustion from lack of sleep and proper food overtook her, she slowly pieced together a plan. Probably a terrible one, as Josephine would later tell her, but a plan nonetheless.

Lucy awoke curled up in a ball on the floor, feigning brokenness wasn't difficult when Evost found her. She made the desperate promised to make an offer of marriage to Lord Blackwell.

Evost was skeptical but loosened the corset—only enough, however, to allow proper breath and a bit more to eat.

When the Aurora stopped moving, preparations for the midway ball began, and Lucy's resolve strengthened.

This would be her only chance—the one time Evost had to let her out of her room. Lucy conjured up the image of the mysterious man in the library, someone whom she wouldn't have minded getting to know more if he had not been a Valtine Lord, and did her best to convince Evost that she truly meant to propose.

Considering the pain she felt, she almost wondered if it would be the better choice. If she went through with the engagement, this would all be over.

Getting ready took an obscene amount of time. If she'd thought the corset would be removed, she was mistaken. She took her regular ice bath with the corset on. They expertly covered the dark circles under her eyes and erased all signs of torture from her face.

Instead of the plain dresses she'd been wearing on the Nova-Manor, Lord Daye sent her a beautiful gown, with a note telling her how proud he was. If he knew the torture she was enduring, he didn't mention it.

The gown was a smoky blue. It had little gems that changed colour and looked as though smoke was rippling from her toes to her hip.

Nothing could hide the fact that she had lost weight. The seamstresses scrambled to take in a stitch here and there so it fit.

Her hair was curled to flow over her shoulders, and a tiara dipped in silver-blue was securely fastened on top of her head.

The midway station balls or parties were always her favourite—this should have been a magical night.

When she entered the ballroom, she wished she could enjoy it. It was one of the most beautiful events she'd ever seen. The dome was fully open to the sparkling darkness above. The Corina Nebula was on full display beyond the chandeliers, which hung high above their heads. A fountain of champagne ran into a river of bubbles as it flowed down the centre table of sweets and confections topped by swirled candies and thick frosting.

Floating stars lit the inside of the dome and cast beautiful shadows and streams of light around the dancers. The full orchestra played from a huge open balcony overlooking the guests, and footmen in navy suits wandered the room, seeing to every need.

It was beautiful. Guests from not only Valtine but all over the hex-system filled the room, although the Valtine lords and ladies did their best to distinguish themselves.

Lucy closed her eyes for a moment, taking in the glorious sound of voices not her own.

Lord Daye was quick to come up beside her. He wore all black and had toned down from his usual flair. He smiled in approval at her appearance.

"You look like the lady I always imagined you would be," he said, kissing her on the cheek, expecting her to like the compliment. Leading her across the floor, he steered her away from the table of cupcakes. Her stomach rumbled when the scent of peppermint and chocolate hit her.

He wasted no time in leading her through the crowd and right to Lord Blackwell. She'd known it would happen soon but had hoped to have a few more minutes to adjust her plan if needed. Blackwell wore a black suit with the smallest hint of the smoked crystals on his long lapel. A black cape wrapped around his shoulders. His dark hair was fashionable, and his smoky blue eyes matched Lucy's gown.

Everyone in the room watched as he bowed over her hand. He raised it, turned her wrist, and kissed it.

A heated blush rushed to her cheeks. His eyes roamed over her and took a little too long to reach her own. She stared straight ahead, unblinking at his unreadable expression. Was he truly a friend? Or was he in league with Evost and Lord Daye? She had so many questions.

Under the gaze of the beaming matrons and couples, Lord Blackwell took her to the dance floor.

This was what everyone wanted, what he wanted. Stability —a couple who would unite the powerful families on Valtine. Who could continue the Idex line of the Daye family in a respectable way.

No scandals, no disappearances. Lots of children. It wasn't really so wrong to want those things. Lucy looked at the dancing guests, their fears and relief united. They had homes, children, and staff who all depended on society staying as it was. But would so much change? If she could be herself, would it really be such a terrible thing? Why couldn't they have both?

Lucy had become so accustomed to the tightness and restrictions that she almost forgot the corset until he put his hand on her waist. A jolt shot through her as the pain summoned her suppressed anger. Lucy was rarely angry at anyone, but now she felt it. Fiery anger bubbled under her skin. Evost had tried to break her, Lord Daye had applauded it, and now Lord Blackwell and everyone else in the room would benefit from her surrender. They would see that a lady only needed a little instruction. All was well, and life would continue on as it always had.

But all was not well. And deep down they knew it. She knew she was giving up on going home and that this next move would send her back to Valtine.

She faltered a little. He spread his hand wide over her back, then ran it lower to rest on her side as the music began to play. The intimate movement signalled his claim on her, but his hand position put the least amount of pressure on the corset. Despite his severe stance, his movements remained slow, his arms strong, holding her in perfect formation. She felt like a broomstick the way he carried her, her toes barely dusting the floor.

Dizzy, Lucy closed her eyes. It was the closest to weightlessness she'd ever been—and disregarding the pain, she momentarily forgot who she was dancing with and what was expected of her.

"What did they do to you?" Worry laced his whisper.

Lucy's eyes opened wide. "Nothing. They didn't do anything," she said, then turned her head to watch the other couples glide around them, holding back the tears, unsure why she couldn't tell him.

"I'm sorry, Lucy. We all play our parts, and I've played mine terribly. Please let me explain. If I'd known—" He spun her slowly under the chandeliers. The lights twinkling off the gems on her dress cast a sparkle onto Lord Blackwell's arm. "I knew your uncle desired a match between us. My involvement with him was purely business, but he fixated on it, and I couldn't dissuade him. Once I found out about the corset, I decided to give him hope. I thought they would leave you alone and let us go back to Orion."

"You said we had an understanding, thinking it would lessen their involvement?" Lucy asked. He adjusted his hand, causing a ripple of pain. Lucy winced, and he put it back down, his fingers gently pushing at the sides of her dress to find the best place to hold her.

He slowed to a stop at the edge of the dance floor, his eyes studying her intently. Brows drawn together, he seemed to be considering what he would tell her. She met his gaze. Nothing masked the distress in his eyes. "It's a bit more complicated than that. I have other reasons for going to Orion, and for befriending Lord Daye. But yes. I misjudged how badly Lord Daye wants this match."

Lucy looked away and smiled at Zandra. The girl wore a stunning red gown. Her hand trembled as she gave Lucy a side wave. Sophia did the same—then looked straight ahead. How many of them were consumed by the fear of others? What had been their breaking point? Would this go on and on, generation after generation?

"If you ask me to marry you, I'll say yes. I would do anything to ease your pain," Lord Blackwell said earnestly. And she believed him. But Lord Blackwell would be stuck in a marriage he'd never intended, and Valine would continue to perpetuate this torture.

She had no true control over the lands she was going to inherit, or the court and their ridiculous rules. She couldn't even guarantee she would make it home—in fact, this next choice might prove she couldn't. Because the one part she could play was to not let Evost win. It was a small part—but dancing, having the whole of the room waiting for her to propose—it was everything.

The music slowed to an end. This was the moment. Her heart sped quickly, as if she still twirled around the room. All eyes were on her. Evost stood off to the side, a wicked smile spread across her usually stoic face. A few guests glared hopefully, while others took more subtle side glances—as if a grand love story played out in front of them.

"I'm sorry, I can't. Not if she wins. And you said it yourself —you're far too old for me," Lucy said, trying to make light of the situation.

"Not much older."

"Age isn't always measured in years." Lucy bit back a tear, knowing it wouldn't take much to sway her. Her heart twisted, and pain clouded her thoughts.

"Right now, you look ancient. I can bring you back to your

father, who can help sort this out. Think about what will happen if you don't."

She knew he was being kind, and meant what he said. She had thought of what would happen if she didn't. And that was the problem.

"You're sweet, but I can't agree to marry you for your kindness. Don't worry, I won't ask you to help with this next part."

Searching the crowd, she found Jasper. He wore all black without a hint of trim. His dark hair was pulled back from his face, and he looked perfectly dangerous. She shot him a pleading look, which he answered immediately and headed in her direction. Couples were resetting for the next dance, still trying to see what would happen.

Lord Blackwell looked sad but didn't protest again as he respectfully released his hold on her, giving her a bit of space between them. He took another step back as Jasper reached them.

"Lord Terrington. Can I have this dance?" Lucy said. He exchanged a look with Lord Blackwell, then held out his arm.

She had not made the expected offer of marriage to Lord Blackwell, and everyone knew it. He retreated to the side of the ballroom.

Lucy winced, then let Jasper put his arm around her.

"I need you to do me a favour," she whispered. "I'm wearing a corset meant to kill. I can't breathe, and I'm in extraordinary pain—stop looking like that, I can take care of myself. I need you to dance with me like nothing is wrong. I want to get the attention of everyone in this room—hopefully Evost and my uncle are watching. And if I pass out, I need you to keep dancing."

"You want me to swing you around the floor like a puppet even if you're not conscious?" He raised a brow, and a glimmer of something dangerous flickered behind his eyes.

"Fine—if I'm dead, you may stop," Lucy smiled up at him, giving him her most dazzling smile.

"This will hurt you."

"Very much," Lucy said and squared her jaw.

<h1 style="text-align:center">Eighteen</h1>

When the scandalous dance between the infamously dark Lord Terrington and heiress Lady Lucy finished, he led her through the crowd and past the throng of guests. Lucy was barely able to stand and when they reached a safe distance, Jasper half carried her toward the guest suites. When they reached the empty halls, maids and butlers poked their heads out of the rooms. They were all waiting for the guests to arrive, ready with hot baths and snacks. One look from Jasper, and they closed the doors quietly.

Lucy didn't ask where he was taking her; she didn't care. She'd won. She had caught sight of Evost's horrified face twice during the dance, once when Jasper spun her and the second time when he had dipped her low enough that her curls tickled the floor. If Lord Blackwell had stayed to watch, she hadn't seen him.

"I thought you were exaggerating—he's going to kill me," Jasper muttered.

An enormous set of double doors with black handles loomed at the end of the hallway. Jasper leaned her against the wall, unlocked the door, then helped her inside.

It was mostly dark, but glowing silver light ran along the floor. The room was lathered in soft greys and sparkling silver trim. A large bed was enclosed with side rails that curved like a comet arching across the night sky. It smelled like jasmine and pine and a mysterious forest.

In the centre of the room was a cluster of overly stuffed chairs. Jasper helped Lucy sit down. She tucked her legs under and arched her arms over the back of the mid-height chair to gain some relief. The pain circled around like barbed wire burning into her ribs. She let silent tears fall and did her best to breathe as little as possible.

She turned her head to look at Jasper. His usual calm broke.

"I am far too old for you—and I consider you as nothing more than a friend—and I would never do anything to harm you."

"Please, say what you need to," Lucy begged. Her ribs burned like they were going to melt in a fire of pain.

"We need to get the dress off so I can see the corset."

"Oh, is that all? Don't worry, I have layers of skirts on, but I don't think I can move—you'll have to cut it off." Lucy closed her eyes again. Waiting for the pain to stop. Even sitting perfectly still, she still felt it vibrate through every nerve in her back, causing a tingling down her arms.

The flick of Jasper's knife echoed in the room. He didn't ask permission again, and she didn't care as he slid the blade carefully into the well-fitted jewelled dress. Smokey beads popped from the torn threads and clattered to the floor. Lucy looked down at the silver bobbles now resting on Jasper's shoes. They were exquisite shoes—with black trim stitched around the base—and they shone like a midnight sea.

"Please don't throw up on them," Jasper mumbled as the top layer of her gown, and then the second, puddled onto the chair, exposing the black net corset underneath.

A stream of swear words burned through her ears. She didn't recognize a few and wondered if he'd picked them up on the outer planets… and if he would teach them to her. They sounded much angrier than the common Valtine words.

He tried to set his blade under the edge, like she had, but to no avail. "I've never seen anything like this. I'm going to call Evost and force her to take this off you. I'm going to kill Lord Daye. I'm going to—I don't know what to do." His defeated tone made her breath quicken, and the pain burst through her. She'd known her plan would hurt, but she didn't understand why the pain wasn't stopping.

"Please try. There has to be a way to open it."

Jasper picked up a miniature datapad from the far side of the room, then connected it to the small narrow panel at the bottom of the corset and swore again.

"This is the craziest tech I've ever seen. Merrick or Dr Moss might know what to do—but locating them could take weeks, months even," he mumbled to himself as he worked.

Lucy's head swam, and she tucked away the bit about Dr Moss and Merrick. Something to ask about later. Right now, she couldn't get out. Jasper couldn't get her out.

She might have to crawl back to Evost or her uncle—and beg for forgiveness. She couldn't—wouldn't—do that.

A loud banging sounded at the door. Jasper moved so quickly at the noise that she barely registered he'd gone.

The knock sounded again.

It might be Evost, or her uncle, or anyone. They hadn't exactly been discreet when leaving the ballroom. She'd gotten herself and Jasper into a world of trouble, being alone like this.

"Jasper—open the door. Let me in." Lord Blackwell's voice was muffled through the door.

There was no way to hide the flood of embarrassment as Jasper let him in. The door closed quickly, and there were hushed words between the two men. Lucy buried her puffy eyes in her folded arms and refused to look up. Lord Blackwell would have seen the way she'd danced with Jasper, and her public declaration of defiance against her uncles wishes, and now she was half undressed, hanging over the armrest of an overstuffed chair. She didn't know why she cared so much, but she did not want him to see her like this.

"I didn't know it would be this bad," Jasper said to Lord Blackwell as the men approached her.

"I danced with her for five seconds and knew something was wrong. How could you not know it would be this bad?" Lord Blackwell accused. Not waiting for Jasper's defence, he pulled up a chair behind Lucy. She peeked under her arm and down to where his leg now rested beside hers.

"I need you to be as still as you can," he said softly, balancing the datapad on his leg.

"Have you ever seen anything like this before?" Jasper asked as he paced back and forth.

"Yes," Lord Blackwell answered plainly, then took a moment to elaborate. He seemed to be choosing his words carefully. "It originated as ship tech, but it's been modified for various uses. I've worked with a similar technology, for keeping documents and other valuables hidden. The electrical current that runs through it causes enough alarm that it prevents anyone from getting too close. It works with a person's Idex. I've never seen it adapted to a corset, and it looks as though it's a prototype—probably set to release only with Evost's Idex."

"Evost said she was working on it specifically for me. I think she would rather see me dead than get beat at her own game."

"Is the current capable of killing her?" Jasper asked.

"I don't see why not. It's been pushed past its expected limitations, and the circuits are running continuously. It was not meant to be used in this way."

"Lucy—" Jasper's tone was a low growl.

"I told you if I died, you could stop dancing," Lucy said through tears.

"When you say it as a joke, it doesn't count as the truth," Jasper murmured.

"Just because I was smiling when I said it, doesn't mean I was joking." She mumbled the words into her arms, and Jasper walked away again.

"I need silence to work. This is complicated, and Lucy is going to need some things when it's all done," Lord Blackwell said. His voice was filled with controlled anger. At Jasper or her uncle or both, she wasn't sure.

"I want Josephine, but I have no idea where she is. They might have already sent her home. I haven't seen her all week. She'll know what I need," Lucy said in a half sob, longing for her dear friend to be close by. Lord Blackwells knee brushed against her hip, holding her still.

"I'll find her," Jasper sounded all too eager for a task. "I'm going to lock you in. No one has access to this room. Don't answer if anyone knocks."

"I wasn't planning on it." Lord Blackwell stood and followed Jasper to the door, where they exchanged a quiet word that Lucy couldn't hear.

When Jasper left, Blackwell sat down again. He worked in focused silence. Lucy did her best to withstand the constant pain, feeling every second like she couldn't go on, and yet somehow she did.

Minutes felt like an eternity. Her thoughts bounced from Lady Daye's disappearance and what it would have been like to grow up on Valtine, to Lord Blackwell and the fact that they'd yet to have a real conversation—now that she knew who he was.

"You said you've seen tech like this for securing documents. Is that why you spoke with Lady Daye before she disappeared?" Lucy asked, needing to distract herself from the way his fingers brushed across the bit of exposed skin on her side as he worked.

"Are you sure you're up for this conversation?" he asked.

"Is there a conversation to be had?"

"I'm going to run a diagnostic for a minute. You need to hold perfectly still. If you can do that, I will tell you what I can —but only because I am to blame for this whole situation." He took a deep breath, setting the datapad back down on his leg. Lucy watched it light up and scroll through screens that meant nothing to her.

"My family on the paternal side is responsible for generations of Idex security systems, but not only the scan points or range scanners that can be used from space or the satellites that relay information. We range from the enormous to the miniature. My grandfather designed the Nova-Manor. Its purpose was to provide a place away from Idex control, but when it was co-opted for something else, my grandfather retired early and closed the business. My father was secretly commissioned for safes and security boxes. That's why Lady Daye was talking to me—she was asking questions about security boxes. I didn't give her any information that would cause her disappearance. After she left, someone requested I look into the matter and Lord Daye's affairs. But as far as I can tell, Lord Daye knew nothing of my conversation with his wife, or my family's involvement in security. His interest in me as a prospective husband for you was purely political. I know Jasper discovered some of this information, but I don't know how much he passed on to you. He's not as sneaky as he thinks he is."

This earned a light laugh from Lucy, a laugh she immediately regretted.

"I spent weeks gaining Lord Dayes' trust, but if he is aware of my particular skills, he hasn't made it known. Like I said, I find it hard to believe that I'm simply the most boring—and therefore most suitable—option for you. My family has access to secrets. I suspect fear or greed, or both, are driving your uncle. I just didn't know to what lengths."

"Thank you," Lucy said in response. She still had so many questions but didn't dare move or say more. The tingling had reached her toes, and she didn't want to do anything to prolong the torture. There was a long pause as Blackwell unhooked the datapad from the corset port.

"I think I have it. This should open the circuit. It's likely going to hurt—more than it does right now. This was designed for torture and nothing else."

"Just do it," Lucy said, knowing she wouldn't last long enough to try anything else.

Lord Blackwell placed one hand on the back of her neck, threading his fingers into her hair as he held her still. The heat from his palm tingled down her spine. "I need you to keep absolutely still. I'm going to trip the system in three—two—one."

A rush of searing pain shot up her neck and into the base of her skull. It wrapped around her ribs and shot through her. Her scream was engulfed in agony.

And then it was gone. The back of the corset opened, exposing her back to the air. The netting fell limp like a leaf and landed on the dresses lying underneath her.

Lord Blackwell let out a shaky breath and slowly removed his hand from where it was resting on the base of her neck.

Lucy shuddered and then, unable to contain the torrent of tears, sobbed.

He stood, crossed the room, grabbed a blanket, and gently draped it over her shoulders.

Lucy tugged at the corners, pulling it around herself.

He came around the front side of the chair, knelt down on the floor in front of her, and brushed away a stray piece of hair from her brow. His grey eyes held hers for a moment.

"I'm sorry they did this to you. I gained your uncle's trust by pretending to be interested in you. I thought by suggesting Orion and implying we had an understanding, he would relent. I am so sorry. Whatever I can do to make this right—tell me. I won't make you face this alone."

Now that she could breathe, her lungs felt funny and loose

and achy.

He caught the tears with his thumb as it brushed across her cheek, then stood when the door opened.

Nineteen

Lucy heard Josephine before she saw her. "I thought you were dead—this horrible man told me I had to come with him to help you, and he wouldn't tell me anything."

"I tried—"

"And I asked if you'd died, and he looked like he wanted to kill me. Oh, you look like death. Whose rooms are these? A bit fussy, don't you think? Look at all those shoes. The man who picked me up was so frightful. We snuck all over the ship and doubled back every time I made too much noise because he didn't want us to be followed. I told him, if we didn't want to be followed, we merely needed to take the special servants' passages—they're in every ship. I got what I thought you would need. I refused to follow him unless he helped. I'll never forgive myself for not standing up to Evost, and he clearly has no idea about these things. He scowled at every single maid and butler we passed. But you know they've all been so worried about you, none of them will say a thing. We ran into the captain. He's a kind man—stern and a little ugly. He said he would keep your location a secret for a day, but promised no more. I don't know why the secrecy—no one is looking for you. Although everyone is talking about you and Jasper."

Lucy pulled the blanket tight around her shoulders and propped her elbows on the back of the chair, so she could see everyone.

Lord Blackwell's sleeves were rolled up to his elbows, his top button was undone. Jasper appeared to have run his hands through his hair more than once and Josephine looked like a terrified, angry ball of relief.

Josephine came close to Lucy. An armload of gowns and clothing was tossed onto the chair beside her.

Lord Blackwell grabbed Josephine's hand when she went to touch Lucy's back. She stepped back reluctantly then made herself useful scooping the pile of cut fabric from under her lady—along with the corset.

"Can you fix me something to eat? Although not much. And maybe a drink?" Lucy asked.

Josephine dropped the pile of gathered items onto the floor in a heap, ready to grant Lucy's request. But Jasper was a step ahead of her. He placed a tray on the table between the three chairs. Lucy stared at him wide-eyed—lords did not serve food.

Her maid peered from Lord Blackwell to Lucy. She took a full plate of small sandwiches and cheese and sat across from Lucy.

Lucy ate the cubed pears from the plate in front of her and took sips of wine. The nausea settled some.

"This isn't a picnic. I should go get the medic," Lord Blackwell growled.

"I'll be fine. I just want to rest." She closed her eyes for a minute. Her back still burned and everything hurt.

"You need to see the doctor," Lord Blackwell said again. "And I'm afraid you haven't accomplished anything. Lord Daye is not likely to let this dissuade him. I don't think you fully understand what kind of man he is."

"I never expected it to," Lucy said, weariness setting in. "Tomorrow I will see a doctor, and may be forced to go back to Valtine. But for now, I want to rest."

Josephine stood and, without asking, started setting the large bed as if they hadn't commandeered Jasper's room. It wouldn't be hard to find her, but like Josephine said, no one was looking. Perhaps Evost was—perhaps she hoped Lucy was already dead.

Lord Blackwell gently helped Lucy to her feet, careful to keep the blanket slung over her shoulders. She stood weakly, barely able to balance.

She held onto his arms for a minute and leaned into him, placing her head on his chest. His heart thumped, and he raised a hand, running it through her hair.

"I'm so sorry," Lord Blackwell said.

"It's not your fault. Your plan of an engagement wasn't a bad one. You just underestimated me."

"I promise never to do that again," he said, then helped her to the bed.

She lay down, letting the pillow soak up her tears, and listened as Lord Blackwell and Jasper discussed all the possible ways to deal with Evost and Lord Daye. When they finally decided on waiting until the next day to make a decision, Lucy closed her eyes.

"Don't open this door for anyone. I'll stay in Blackwell's

rooms tonight, and tomorrow we'll decide what needs to be done," Jasper said, clearly not giving up on getting them all to Orion.

Once they were gone, Josephine climbed onto the bed beside Lucy.

"You already have a plan, don't you?" Josephine asked. She arranged the pillows and straightened the blanket a little.

"I do. What dresses did you bring?" Lucy asked. Josephine smiled wickedly and held them up one after the other. Lucy made her decision and fell into a restless sleep.

Morning came too quickly, and Josephine woke Lucy with a start. The room, still cloaked in night, looked larger than before. It would be two hours before everyone was up for breakfast.

Lucy eased her aching body into the bath. The burns from the corset didn't hurt as much, but they left an odd rippling of red up her back and around her sides. She ate everything remaining from the night before, until her stomach ached. Josephine prattled about the staff and the things she'd done over the past week. More than one of the crew had tried to intervene on Lucy's behalf, but there was little anyone could do.

The dark-green gown Lucy had picked for the morning was designed for an evening at the opera. The neck came up high and deep tear-shaped gems buttoned around her neck. The same glittering jewels trimmed the open back. Deep purple marks where the corset had burned her skin glared in contrast. Slits in the floor-length skirts billowed with tulle that overly accentuated her hips.

She hadn't looked prettier in all her time on Valtine.

Lucy held the corset, the smooth black netting like gauze under her fingers, as Josephine brushed her blond hair until it hung golden and gleaming down her back. A single strand of green pearls wound in a circlet on top of her head like a crown. Once Josephine had her dressed, she led her down the back staff stairs and into the exclusive Valtine ladies' breakfast room.

Garlands of white lilies ran along the centre of the table, and vases with lilacs and purple daisies dotted the spaces between.

It was still too early for anyone to be up, but the room smelled like strong coffee. Down the centre of the table, pastries and fresh fruit awaited their consumption. Plates and hot dishes on the sideboard table were steaming and ready to be filled. Enough chairs to host a hundred guests ran the length.

Lucy greeted the staff, who were all watching her in open astonishment and whispering to one another.

"Don't bother whispering—I hope you're saying how utterly insane this is, and that it had better work!"

Around a vase of fresh flowers, Lucy displayed the corset on a cake pedestal—it seemed such a waste to mess with the food. She pulled a few of the flowers out of the vase and set them around it. It almost looked pretty.

Then Lucy sat in the chair across from it to observe every woman who entered the room.

"No going back now," she said as she filled her plate and waited for the young ladies to arrive.

Twenty

The first lady to walk in wore a lovely yellow morning dress. When she saw Lucy, her eyes widened. She took a plate, barely filled it, and requested a coffee. She sat at the far end of the table. As the room slowly filled, not one girl looked Lucy in the eye. They all took their breakfast and risked an occasional glance at the centre of the table where Lucy's corset sat on display.

Zandra arrived in a pale-pink gown, her hair in a braided coil. She took one look at the corset, and then Lucy's gown, and a huge smile spread across her face.

Sophia tried to pull Zandra away, but she shook her hand free and sat down beside Lucy.

"What are you doing?" Zandra asked quietly.

"I'm having breakfast," Lucy replied and took a long drink of coffee.

As the room filled, they chatted easily about the Aurora and the ball. Lucy didn't know polite conversation could be so easy. The spot beside her remained empty until a young girl sat down. Her hands trembled as she stirred her coffee in slow circles.

And then the ripple effect Lucy had hoped for was set in motion. The speed at which the room filled meant the rumours were spreading. There was something going on in the ladies' breakfast room. The latecomers were not fully ready. Hair wasn't completely up and dresses were half laced. Lucy's heart pounded in her chest. She had no idea how this would play out, but she needed to win this one.

When Evost arrived, she embodied a forced calm. She didn't frown or smile or yell. She held herself perfectly still. Not a single muscle in her face twitched. She stood across the table from Lucy, hands clasped firmly behind her back.

"I realize what a trying time we've had. I think it is best if you come with me and leave everyone to their morning."

Her eyes roamed around the table. When they rested on the corset in the middle of the table, a strangled growl escaped her mouth.

"I'm sorry. Did you hear someone talking?" Lucy said to Zandra, who bravely tried not to laugh. "This is a very inappropriate time to get the giggles, Zandra—we're trying to have breakfast. Why don't I get us some lemon-ice? That should sour us back up." Lucy stood and turned toward the buffet table to get the lemons. She made sure to pull her hair over her shoulder, leaving her back bare.

An audible gasp went up from around the room as everyone stared unbelievingly at the purple and red marks.

Lucy kept her back turned and made a show of stretching and picked up a few ices before putting them in a bowl. She did really love the tart-cold confections.

When she turned back, the room had filled to capacity and

faces were peeking in from the doorways.

Alarmed looks and glances darted from Lucy to Evost and back again.

"You did this to yourself. If you'd obeyed, you would have been fine," Evost hissed, and the perfect face cracked just a little. "I want you to reconsider. If you do not follow me out of this room, your reputation will be entirely soiled, and no one will want you."

"I want you to remember. You did this to yourself. My reputation has already been solidified, and you are longer needed."

It was a bold statement. But if all of Valtine clung to her marital status to provide stability, then certainly she had the influence required.

The crowd parted as Evost stomped around the table. Lucy turned to face her and held out a bunch of grapes from the table in front of her. She ignored the feeling that this was not going to work and blocked out the thundering in her chest.

"It's not really losing—Valtine is always following rules because someone with a better Idex than theirs told them to. The thing is, I'm told by everyone that an Idex doesn't get better than mine, so shouldn't we all just move on? Consider this a peace offering," Lucy said, the tiny cluster dangling from her fingers. "I've learned that everyone has a breaking point, and before you hit yours, I suggest you walk away the way a lady should."

Evost smacked the grapes out of her hand. They hit the floor and burst from the vines, rolling in all directions. Grabbing Lucy's arm, she pulled her forward. Lucy didn't know what she meant to accomplish. There was absolutely no way she would be led from the dining room like a child. But Evost's cruelty had lower depths, and she roughly placed a hand on Lucy's back to propel her forward. Although the constant ebb of pain had stopped, the burns were still incredibly sensitive to touch and Lucy cried out.

Without a second thought, Lucy reached for the closest thing and dumped it on Evost's head. Blunut syrup trickled over her face and down her nose, then ambled down the front of her gown.

Evost cracked. She screamed and lunged for Lucy, grabbing a handful of hair. Lucy instinctively reached up to hold the hand and prevent her from ripping out her hair, all the while avoiding the sticky syrup.

"What is the meaning of this?" Lord Daye's voice boomed in the dining room. People pressed back from his looming presence. He was the picture of perfection. Groomed hair and a clean-shaven jaw. A large ruby stud held his morning cravat in place. He didn't look as though he'd been up all night worrying about the welfare of his niece, and he probably hadn't.

Lord Daye stood at the end of the table, Lord Blackwell beside him, both wore unreadable expressions.

The scene was undeniable. Evost had lost all control. She straightened immediately and stammered unintelligibly.

"Explain yourself," Lord Daye said.

"Well, I decided since I was on holiday from hosting, I'd start a new trend of ball gowns at breakfast. I needed the opinion of the other ladies, of course." Lucy did a full twirl, showing her back to the newly arrived guests and causing a second wave of horrified gasps. "Kind of a trial, but to be honest, I don't think it's worth the effort. I do look fabulous no matter what I'm wearing, so perhaps... Oh, I see now you meant Evost—my mistake." Lucy put her hands on her hips and swayed them a little.

Evost stammered, "You said by any means necessary—"

Lucy had little doubt that Lord Daye knew about the torture she'd endured. But now he had to publicly admit to it. She had produced a stalemate of cosmic proportions. She couldn't win, but now he had to lose.

"I meant gowns and bribing her with costly jewels and dance lessons—certainly not whatever this is," Lord Daye said diplomatically. It didn't deny his obvious employment of Evost but absolved him of responsibility.

"This is what it takes to turn out the ladies you find acceptable. This has always been my way of doing things." Evost looked around the table, pleading with the lords and ladies to stand with her.

"No. They don't need torture to know they are capable of nice conversation and delightful parties. They can be kind and sweet and thoughtful. They can be creative and brave." Lucy looked down at Zandra and smiled. "They do not need to be crushed into perfection."

The blunut continued to slink down Evost's dress, pulling at the fabric.

She watched as Lord Daye quickly read the faces and opinions of those around the room, and she did the same. While there were a few whose soured frowns suggested they wanted him to take action against Lucy, the looks of concern and shock outweighed them.

"I will see that you are escorted onto the midway station and sent back to Valtine—your services are no longer required," Lord Daye said, earning a round of applause as if he'd been the one to save the day.

Lucy rolled her eyes.

Lord Blackwell said something quietly to Lord Daye, which seemed to put him at ease. Then Lord Blackwell fixed his attention on her. Their eyes locked from across the room, and her heart flipped. His expression was unreadable, and she resisted the urge to run over to him.

Evost stepped on the grapes, squishing them to the floor and bringing Lucy back to the moment. Back straight and lips pressed together, Evost marched from the breakfast room along with the throng of onlookers. A few of the ladies stood, clearly disapproving of what had transpired, but the majority stayed.

The doors to the ladies' breakfast room closed, and the room exploded with the sound of seventy-five women, cheering, crying, congratulating, and apologizing.

Lucy ordered a round of champagne for the room, despite the early hour. Not a single server declined her request but proudly carried trays with towers of champagne glasses, fresh strawberries, and cheese.

Lucy retold the events of the previous week in detail. The cupcake, the corset, and the dance with Jasper.

"How romantic—" Sophia said, popping a strawberry into her mouth. She leaned over and took three more.

"Not every friendship needs to be romantic."

"But some of them?"

Lucy blushed. She'd tried to push Lord Blackwell out of her mind and said almost nothing of his involvement.

"How did you get out of the corset?" An elderly woman asked, picking the deactivated mess from the cake. She inspected it, her eyes wide. "I've never seen anything like this in all my years."

"I had some help," was all Lucy said, and everyone sighed again.

The morning continued; none of them returned for their regular dressings, or for hair and make-up, or for walks around the ship. If the men wondered where they were, none came to check. News must have travelled to some degree, but what was being said, Lucy had no idea.

Each girl shared her own story of Evost—or of similar situations of forced conformity—although none had pushed back as hard as Lucy had. One night in the corset and most of them learned to not question.

Lucy's heart broke for every one of them.

Twenty-One

Lucy sat with the women past the lunch hour. When another round of food arrived, she snuck out and made her way to the first floor medical bay.

The scent of eucalyptus and lavender infused the soft, glowing lights. Water fountains and hanging plants hung on white walls. It was clean and warm.

After being greeted by a young woman, the medical attendant brought her to a private room to meet with the doctor who recorded and treated her injuries. A cooling balm pulled the lingering burn out, and they documented the damage caused.

The doctor was curious about the pattern of the burns and requested additional scans, which Lucy declined. She didn't want anyone other than her doctor on Orion taking a closer look; she thanked them and made her way back to her rooms.

The pile of clothing from Jasper's room had been brought back and dumped in a heap on the floor. Josephine waited with the bed pulled down. Nix was already sprawled across the centre, fast asleep. Lucy climbed in—disturbing Nix, who meowed loudly— and padded over. She snuggled in and slept soundly.

A full day passed. The Aurora remained at the midway station—delayed. She learned from Jasper that, despite the captain's sympathies to her plight, Lord Daye had ordered the Aurora to remain indefinitely. It was one of those moments where Lucy remembered how much power her uncle wielded. She didn't blame the captain for not wanting to risk his cargo or crew by going against Lord Daye's orders. There had been little hope that Lord Daye would see reason—it was a risk she'd taken when she defeated Evost.

The following afternoon she met with Jasper and Lord Blackwell in a private lounge, away from the obsessive stares of the other guests. Lucy had another impossible choice before her. Lord Blackwell had offered a marriage agreement that they would end once they reached Orion. And Jasper was practically begging her to take it.

"I'm sorry, Jasper, but I swore I would never marry a Valtine lord. Perhaps it's time to accept that Lady Daye is gone and that I can't help you find her," Lucy said.

"I understand not wanting to let your uncle win, but we can find a way out of the marriage to Blackwell. You just heard him. He's agreed to not force you to marry once the engagement is set."

It was tempting now that they were working together, but engagements were not easily broken.

"And why are you agreeing to this?" Lucy asked Lord Blackwell. "A broken engagement is not a simple matter, and I think this goes beyond feeling responsible for Lord Daye's excessive measures."

"I still have my own reasons for reaching Orion, but as I said before, I would do anything to help you out of this mess. What do you think will happen when you return to Valtine and Lord Daye sets his sights on some other gentleman? I know you're strong and incredibly brave, but you don't deserve to be treated like this. Let me help you. Please."

Lucy wavered for a moment, considering her options, when Jasper interjected again.

"I also uncovered some disturbing information from my incoming messages on the midway station. Lord Daye has already halted all attempts to find Lady Daye. And it's rumoured his efforts to find her were all a grand show… using ambassadors to check places where lots of people would see and hear them. No one is looking for her. Please—I need your help."

Lucy mulled over his words, and in the end she was persuaded. Someone should be searching for her aunt. Lord Blackwell had agreed to a fake engagement, although getting out of a marriage agreement was tricky. Especially on Orion. An engagement was as good as a legal contract, and breaking one could have both financial and legal implications. Valtine might have some ridiculous rules, but on Orion, your word and your promise were everything.

"Whatever secrets you both are hiding—and for pity's sake, it's incredibly obvious that you are—I want you to know I'm doing this for my aunt. Guarantee I won't have to marry Blackwell, even if it means running away with Jasper." Lucy took a long drink of iced tea, enjoying the look on Jasper's face at the thought of having to run away with her. She was satisfied he would hold up his end of the bargain. She was almost sad when Lord Blackwell didn't look even the least bit hurt—but he'd never intended to marry her, anyway. As they talked over the details of the plan, Lord Blackwell brought up a good point.

"Although it might be for nothing. After everything that has happened, I think it unlikely Lord Daye will accept you just agreeing to marry me. You put up a great fight."

Lucy thought for all of thirty seconds, quickly coming up with a plan. She reassured them both that she had just the thing to convince Lord Daye that the engagement was real and that they could depart for Orion together.

The following morning, a sharply dressed crew member guided her to the Valtine morning room. Opal-lined walls sparkled beneath a pearl-studded ceiling.

A black teapot sat on the table with two silver glasses where Lord Daye was having tea. He added a cube of sugar and stirred, then waited a moment so no one would notice and added another. Lucy rolled her eyes—no one cared how much sugar he had. She almost pitied the man who couldn't even enjoy breakfast without thinking about others' opinions.

Before she lost her nerve, Lucy sat down across from him.

"It is time to move on to Orion. We cannot stay at the midway forever," she said, letting the water pour from the black spout and into the teacup. "I am ready to go home, and I am sure you are ready for the same. Can we not part ways here—peacefully?"

"You are an insignificant fool," he said, venom pouring from the mask of stone he wore. He clearly was not in a peaceful mood. "This victory of yours against Evost will change nothing."

"I agree—I am insignificant, and I'm not worth the trouble."

Lord Daye stirred angrily. "I do not know what you hope to accomplish. You cannot change Valtine. It has been this way for hundreds of years."

"I don't want to change Valtine. It has entertainment and balls and parties and dresses. I love to dance. The staff are always well cared for, no one wants for food or shelter. Valtine is beautiful—I wouldn't change a thing. But for all its beauty and perfection, it is a cage, and you are stuck inside just as much as anyone else. I will never understand why people who have everything, every happiness and freedom, would add so much weight to their lives. The desire to control others is beyond me. Your so-called perfection comes at a cost I'm not willing to pay."

Lord Daye sneered. "I pity you, because one day you will look back on your life and see how extraordinary you could have been,"

"I doubt it. I'm pretty amazing." Lucy added three extra sugars to her tea and let the cubes bobble before they melted into the dark liquid. "I guess we're stuck here at the midway for eternity. Valtine won't change, and neither will I. But there are smaller problems keeping us here. There is no way Lord Blackwell will even look in my direction after the chaos I've caused. You are holding an entire ship captive for something that will never happen, even if I did my best right now."

"I can assure you—the allure of your wealth and power and family status would sway anyone. You forget that, unlike you, I've spent a considerable amount of time in Lord Blackwell's company. He'll leap at the chance to marry you. Valtine will see him as a hero, taking you in hand; and this week will be brushed away as if it never happened. Which is what you do not understand. Those in control like to keep it that way, and your antics will not change anything."

On cue, Lord Blackwell entered from the opposite end of the room. He was handsome. Clean cut and polite. Not shy, but not bold either. A silver crest pin held the morning cloak that folded over his shoulder, revealing a dark-green shirt underneath.

"I'll prove it to you that Lord Blackwell will reject me." Before Lord Daye could stop her, she flounced across the room to where Lord Blackwell stood. She took her time to curtsy low, getting the attention of everyone in the room.

"Lord Blackwell—" she said with more elegance than she felt. It was a ruse, but one she'd never imagined playing. She was going to propose. This was for Lady Daye, and for Jasper, and to get home, she reminded herself. It had to appear real. "I would like to, in the presence of my uncle, ask you to join the Daye family and marry me."

She looked back at her uncle, who maintained a mask of stone.

A tingle from her fingers startled Lucy as Lord Blackwell took her hand. She turned back to face him and saw that he'd stepped closer. He was looking at her, his eyes soft and warm. Lucy's heart thundered loudly. His fingers closed over her hand and he lifted her wrist and kissed the inside. This is how she'd imagined a genuine proposal to go. The way he was looking at her... the way he kissed her. For a moment she forgot the guests. She forgot her uncle and the fact that this was all for show. A rush of heat turned her cheeks pink, and she bit her bottom lip.

"I have been living in anticipation of you asking me. I accept," he replied. His low voice sent a thrill down her spine.

A hush fell over the crowd. There was a soft pattering of hands clapping. Lord Blackwell didn't release her hand, and her heart didn't stop thundering. Lord Daye rose, accepted congratulations from around the room, and made his way to the newly engaged couple.

"I am happy for you," Lord Daye gloated, as if he'd won a grand tournament. "I have always—only—wanted what was best for you. I shall inform the captain that we may proceed to Orion, where I will stay until the marriage takes place."

Twenty-Two

Nothing could dampen Lucy's mood as they crept closer to Orion, not even Jasper's intense restlessness.

"This ship moves too slowly," he said as they sat on the grand pool deck. Lucy stretched out under the warm sunlamps, dreaming of real sunshine.

"There is nothing we can learn or do until we reach Orion. Your stressing won't change the timeline, and I hate to remind you, but there's a good chance we'll fail. I can't imagine we can find my aunt when no one else has been able to."

Jasper's look of determined misery stopped Lucy from continuing. He ran his hand through his hair, then picked up the blade again.

"Can you teach me how to spin my knife?" Lucy asked, watching the blades whirl around like a windmill in a tornado.

He leapt at the distraction.

After five minutes of instruction, Lucy could flip the knife back and forth, but still dropped it frequently.

"Everything else is built on muscle memory. Keep doing this, and then I'll show you some tricks."

"Oh, this is fun—I can see why you do it. So I have to ask—what's the story between you and Lady Daye?"

Jasper leaned back and closed his eyes, blocking her out.

"It might help to talk about it. I find talking always improves my mood. And we have another week to go. Who knows, perhaps you'll tell me something useful."

Lucy gazed over the pool and watched the ripples of the water as swimmers glided past them.

"There isn't much to tell. There was a time when I would have been much like your uncle if I'd continued down the path I was on. My family has great influence in the Valtine courts. Even now, my income remains undiminished despite my time away, and no matter how much I spend, I always have more. My mother was incredibly wise in investments and new technologies. When I met Lady Daye, I was young and loved extravagant parties. We had the best of everything and spent an entire year enjoying court together. The whole time I thought we were falling in love, but she was already engaged to Lord Daye. I didn't find out until a week before the wedding. I was lovestruck—declared I would marry her and take her away. She didn't even consider my plan. There were things more important to her than love. Heartbroken, I asked for a commission on the outer planets. I left like a child running away from home. It's funny, because I went on believing I was better than everyone else and was going to prove it to the universe. I met Captain Merrick—my cousin, of course. He saved my life more than once."

"Do you still love her?" Lucy clasped her hands to her chest, sticking her thumb with the forgotten blade. She dropped it between the chairs.

Jasper picked it up and passed it back to her, inspecting the small nick on her thumb. "I don't even know her."

"But you would cross the planets to find her?"

"Yes, I'd do anything to track her down."

Lucy took her hand back and closed up her knife for the day. She leaned back in the chair. Jasper's declaration was truly the most romantic thing she'd ever heard. She couldn't imagine anyone crossing anything for her.

* * *

Later, in the middle of the night, Lucy caught Lord Blackwell wandering the halls. She quickened her pace and joined his side.

"I've slept so much the past few days. Now I'm wide awake. I don't mind, though. I've never been one to keep a normal schedule," Lucy said by way of greeting. The official engagement made it all awkward. How did one behave with a fake fiancé? Apparently, he was having an easier time accepting their situation and casually walked closer to her so that their shoulders brushed.

"You've recovered, then?" he asked, concern etched between his eyes. She couldn't help but wonder what he truly thought of her. He was a quiet man—the first time she'd met him, he was sitting in the dark by himself.

"I'm fine. Are you okay? I know you don't love travelling and being off planet."

"The captain has been very understanding and has provided me with unique accommodations."

They reached a lift and got in together. The doors closed,

and Lucy was acutely aware of how little room there was as they descended two floors.

"We should probably have a plan. I'm not sure how to do this, but we should be seen together at least once a day—and maybe have dinner together?"

Lord Blackwell stiffened, and she wondered if she was asking too much. The lift stopped, and when Lucy made no move to follow him, Lord Blackwell stepped out.

"I will see you tomorrow, then."

He disappeared as the doors closed, leaving Lucy alone inside.

The brief encounter left her sitting with uncomfortably pleasant feelings. The mysterious man from the study and this self-assured Valtine lord clashed in her mind yet also made perfect sense.

It was like meeting a person for the first time who she already knew.

Every day, they walked the ship's halls, as planned, and then sat down to dinner with various people they'd met. Lucy soon realized that she was making fewer smiling faces out of flowers and was actually enjoying her time with Lord Blackwell.

More than enjoying… she wasn't bored.

There was nothing exceptional about him. He didn't tell extravagant stories or entertain everyone. It was the little things. The way he'd hide a smile when someone said something ridiculous, or remember what Lucy was talking about. She didn't even remember half the things she said, and no one had ever listened to her long enough to ask questions. He didn't sit and linger at the table, and Lucy liked the polite way he stood and offered his arm to her before they'd walk the halls. He was restless on the ship, but it was a controlled restlessness. He was different from her in every way, and yet the time they spent together fit.

They were only two days from Orion when Lucy met Lord Blackwell on the mid-deck for their usual walk and informed him of the news. Nix escaped.

Josephine was unconsolable even though Lucy wasn't blaming her. Nix didn't like staying in his room, and it wasn't as if he knew the rules of the Aurora.

"Change of plans. We need to find Nix," Lucy stated, wrapping his arm around hers. She leaned in against him and noticed the slightest hint of lavender and mint. She wanted to press her face into his shoulder and see if the lovely scent went all the way to his skin but controlled herself. "He's escaped again, and one of the rules given to me was that he must stay with Josephine. We can just wander up and down the halls. If Nix is around, he'll come out. He's not the type to hide away."

"Listen to you talking about rules," he teased.

"And this is why everyone misjudges me. I am actually all for rules. A cat can cause a lot of trouble on a ship. Also, guild law makes sense, especially for the dead. If someone disappears, their business is held intact for ten years before transferring." Lucy cringed at her choice of topic.

"And if someone came back after ten years and a day?"

"Then the guilds would meet and decide if it's reasonable to overrule the rule. This law also prevents a person from killing someone to get their inheritance. The body would need to be left in plain sight instead of dumping it somewhere. But of course you know that, and this is a dreary conversation for a morning walk."

"Why does morning make a conversation acceptable or dreary?"

"Coffee, and the lack of consumption," Lucy said decidedly. Lord Blackwell agreed, and they stopped to procure steaming cups of black coffee.

"Now that our coffee situation is resolved, we should probably talk about happier things. I've been thinking about how to break off our engagement, and even though we've spent nearly every day together, I still know so little about you —and I doubt I can use your corset-adjusting abilities against you. I need at least three valid reasons to make me walk away from the engagement."

They rounded a corner and smiled at the other hall wanderers. Life on the Aurora had become monotonous for many. With no sign of Nix, they headed to the lower decks.

"You're right—this is a much happier conversation," Lord Blackwell said dryly. "Well, to start with, I'm quite a bit older than you."

"Right. How old are you?"

"Twenty-nine."

"Four years between us is hardly enough to call you old."

"I thought age wasn't measured in years?"

"No—but not everyone thinks like we do."

"I don't like space travel," he said and shrugged. Lucy eyed him. He did look tired as he took a long drink of the black liquid.

"I'm sorry. The end of space travel must feel even longer for you. I enjoy the various cargo ships, but I get terribly impatient, so no one would believe I called off our wedding because you dislike space travel," Lucy countered. They entered a small theatre. Hundreds of empty chairs were lined in perfect rows that arched around the centre stage. A maid was sweeping, and another polished the brass railings. Neither paid Lord Blackwell any attention.

"I'm a terrible kisser," he said, one hand gliding over the curved backs of the seats.

Lucy almost tripped on the even red carpet and had to steady her coffee. He steadied her with one hand under her arm.

Taking a moment to collect herself, she noticed his grin. He was definitely in a teasing mood this morning.

"Is that why you wouldn't kiss me in the study?" The quip was too slow and came out unnaturally.

"Obviously," he replied. If he noticed her fluster, he didn't call her out on it, making her feel much braver. They climbed up the shiny wood plank stairs and walked across the stage.

"Wait—how do you know you're bad at kissing? Who provides that kind of information? Who says, *Oh, thank you so much for kissing me, but you're really not any good at it?* You just said that so I'd ask you to kiss me and prove it."

"If I was trying to get you to kiss me, I wouldn't play games. No one should be tricked into kissing."

Lucy's head swam. Somehow they'd stumbled back onto the topic of kissing, and it was as if they were back in the study—except this time she hadn't been the one to bring it up.

"What would you do, if you were trying to get me to kiss you?"

They stopped at the back of the stage, and he opened a door

between two large racks of brightly coloured fabric sheets. He turned to face her. Lucy took a step back until she could lean against the open door, her palms flat against the rough panel. He took a step closer to her, his eyes focused on hers. Her stomach felt like she was trying to do somersaults underwater. He leaned in close.

"I would tell you I've been thinking about you every day since we met, and the only thing that makes endless weeks in space bearable is the moments I spend with you."

It sounded like a true confession, and Lucy almost forgot the whole thing was a ruse. He closed the distance, and Lucy leaned forward to breathe in the clean scent again.

Lord Blackwell stepped back as Nix pounced on her feet and meowed loudly, breaking the moment. Lucy scowled at the cat, then looked quizzically at Lord Blackwell.

"He was staying in my room—" Lord Blackwell said guiltily.

Lucy's heart pounded as she picked up her cat and snuggled him. The open door behind her revealed a large room with ceilings three stories high. With no productions scheduled for this voyage, it was a perfectly cozy room tucked away from the rest of the guests.

"Why didn't you tell me he was here?"

"What, and miss the opportunity to walk you through the whole ship, talking about reasons to end our engagement?"

His expression was completely unreadable.

"We've now accomplished two objectives. Our obligatory time together has been completed—and you have Nix and so are no longer a rule breaker. Did you want me to walk you back to your room?"

Nix wiggled as if he wanted to stay where he was instead of

returning with Lucy. She scratched the top of his head until he calmed in her arms. Perhaps bringing a cat everywhere wasn't the best idea. "I'm not going back to my room—as promised, I need to bring Nix to Josephine."

She looked up and her eyes met his, holding his gaze as she swallowed a lump. He looked unsettled at her rejection, and Lucy cursed herself for being so quick to speak. She's missed her opportunity to have him walk her back.

"Until tomorrow, then." He bowed slightly. A sound over her shoulder made her turn away, and when she looked back, he'd quietly closed the door before she could fix her mistake.

The worst part was, she *knew* it was a mistake.

Twenty-Three

Every day leading up to Orion felt longer than the one before. Lucy could have sworn the captain had shifted the timing—the days felt endless, and it seemed they were never going to make it.

When they finally arrived, syncing orbit dragged into eternity, and the shuttles loaded at a snail's pace.

Lucy sat beside Lord Blackwell. An extra seat had been allotted between him and Lord Daye. It was a waste of space, making other guests wait even longer to disembark. Josephine sat holding Nix in the back section with the other staff.

If Lord Daye was nervous about facing her father after what had transpired with Evost, it didn't show. She wondered if he took any responsibility at all, or if he even cared.

Lord Blackwell looked equally unconcerned about meeting her father, Alarik.

Her father was not going to like the idea of a fake engagement. Lucy turned her nose up at the ridiculous rules of decorum, yet understood full well from the guilds how much weight a person's word carried. They'd been unable to imagine a reasonable excuse, making it all the more difficult. Going back on a promise, especially a promise of marriage, was not in good character. Guild strength was built on honouring that.

The shuttle finally descended, leaving the Aurora behind but transporting them toward a new set of problems ahead.

Lucy gripped Lord Blackwell's hand tightly. A bubbling in her chest filled her with a longing so powerful, she wanted to reach through the hull of the shuttle and pull the planet to her.

She was home.

She tugged at the buckles the moment they landed, although they refused to release until all the safety checks were completed. The moment the doors opened, Lucy sped past the waiting attendants and sprinted from the docks.

Cool mountain air rushed through her hair, tousling it into a flurry of blond curls.

Viceroy Alarik stood at the end of the stone tunnel, waiting for his daughter. She threw herself at him, letting him take the full brunt of her joy.

"Ooph," he said, catching and squeezing her tightly. He was big and burly and so gentle as he picked her up. She brushed a tear off his cheek and kissed one side, then the other, as he set her down.

He was a large man, with black hair pulled back in a tight knot. She noticed a sprinkling of more grey than she remembered. The lines beside his eyes crinkled as a smile reached her heart. He stood back, composed, and not at all embarrassed by the show of emotion. Then he turned to greet the other guests as they disembarked at a more reasonable pace.

Alarik clasped Lord Daye's hand and shook it. "Thank you

for bringing my daughter home—and for your regular updates on how she was doing. They were most informative. I was surprised to learn you would accompany her here."

"It was my pleasure," Lord Daye said. He pulled his hand back and wiped it with a scarf.

"Josephine, nice to see you again too." Alarik winked at Lucy's maid, who blushed.

Lord Blackwell took his time joining the party. Alarik narrowed his gaze, not missing a beat.

"This must be your fiancé. Welcome to Orion." Alarik held out his hand.

Fiance, which meant Alarik already knew. Lord Blackwell took Alarik's hand and shook it briefly.

Lucy glared at her uncle. "I'm sorry. I wanted to tell you in person. I didn't realize Lord Daye would send news ahead, or I would have written myself."

"I'm sure you will tell me all about it once we've settled in," Alarik said, then made a grand gesture of ushering them away from the docks and into the warmth of the castle. Glorious large stones in perfect symmetry towered up to the clouds in grand archways, turrets, and balconies. Lucy was home, and she wasn't going to allow Lord Daye to ruin it.

The following morning, Lucy sat in the private breakfast room with Alarik. It felt like years since she'd had a moment alone with her father. The table had a yellow cloth placed over it. Fancy plates with hand-painted blooms were accompanied by crystal mugs full of steaming, froth-topped coffee.

The small sitting area overlooked the vibrant village. Houses and shops wound through the valley and up the mountainside.

In the centre was a large hub, where shuttles flew in and out.

Sweet mountain air blew in through an open window and whispered through her hair.

What she'd noticed when she first docked was now clear: Alarik had aged in the year she'd been away. The small lines beside his eyes were deeper, and his face was harder. His cozy morning jacket slanted over his hard shoulders.

"It's good to be home with you," Lucy said. She reached across the table and held his hand.

"Did you have a pleasant time?" he asked, searching her face. She wanted to confide all the hardships, but the words stuck. She knew he would blame himself for letting her go, and yet she didn't want to lie. In the short time she'd been home, she'd already noted that the meeting and council rooms were open and full. A summit was happening, and Alarik was trusted with overseeing all the pre-summit meetings. Her heart swelled with pride at the way he cared for and conducted the affair; her troubles could wait until the summit was over.

"There were many wonderful things—but I wouldn't want to live there."

This declaration seemed to unsettle him, and Lucy recalled how relieved he had been when she'd first gone to live with Lord Daye. Perhaps he was unhappy to have her back.

Unfortunately, before she could ask him what he truly felt—and clear up the situation about Lord Blackwell—Lord Daye joined them.

"Clarence, nice to see you," Alarik said icily. Gone was the former politeness. The use of his first name made Lucy giggle. No one dared to call Lord Daye *Clarence*.

He filled his plate with the perfect portions of each item and had the audacity of a Valtine lord to sit down with them uninvited.

As if Lord Daye had perfectly timed his interruption, one of the castle guards appeared. "Sorry to intrude—the Ambassador from Corva has some questions regarding tables for tomorrow's meetings."

Alarik stood, looking weary of the ordeal before it had even started. He bowed to them both and followed the guard out.

Lucy made a show of stirring in three more spoonfuls of sugar and took a sip of the syruped coffee. "I can't imagine why you've stayed. I'm marrying Lord Blackwell. What more could you want?"

"I'm making sure you are married before I leave. I've already secured the document on the Aurora and set a date for six weeks. All as your *doting* uncle, I assure you. And before you protest, I'm not an ignorant man—I know you're keeping company with Jasper. I've seen you two together and the way he leers at you."

Lucy spit out her coffee, then shook the drips off her toast before taking a bite.

He dabbed the imaginary splashing off the back of his hand.

"Don't be ridiculous. Jasper is Lady Cristelle's friend, which makes him my friend. His cousin is likely to marry Lady Cristelle. There is nothing more between us than friendship, I assure you." It irked her that he'd gotten the wrong idea.

"Lord Terrington isn't the type to have friends. And if you were previously unaware, this cousin of his is no more a relative than Josephine. Who do you think turns cousins into lords? Who do you think has control of every secret, every update on the system? I'll see to it that Lady Cristelle's fiancé is shown as the imposter he is if Jasper gets between you and Lord Blackwell."

Lucy leaned back. The threat carried a tinge of humour seeing as she had zero affection for Jasper, and it hardly put Lady Cristelle's future on the line—Lady Cristelle could hold her own against Lord Daye or anyone else. But it still felt like spiders under her skin that he'd even consider threatening her in her father's house.

"Are you admitting you can tamper with Idex coding? I didn't think it was possible—or legal." Lucy took a large bite of her toast and smiled as she chewed.

She looked at her uncle. Power. He was in a position to make changes to Idex happen. Lucy wondered if Jasper knew and if that information mattered to him at all.

Lord Daye took two perfectly sized bites and leaned over the table. "I don't know what game you are playing, but you will heed my words."

"As far as I can tell, the only one playing games is you, and the last person to say something similar to me was let off on a midway station." Lucy threw out a veiled threat of her own. Before Lord Daye could retaliate, Alarik returned with the Ambassador and a few other dignitaries. He looked apologetically at Lucy. She smiled sweetly at him and stayed long enough for him to know she didn't resent the interruption at all.

Twenty-Four

The next two days continued in a blur of one activity after the other. With little chance of getting time alone with her father, Lucy plunged into her quest for answers about Lady Daye and her disappearance. She'd talked to everyone at the castle and found she had little trouble getting information.

Midafternoon on the third day, Lucy stood in the centre of her room on a pedestal. A bolt of pink-and-plum fabric was draped over one shoulder and a dark black silk over the other. She held up a soft-green between the two and tucked it under her chin, tilting her head and looking into the mirror as the seamstress pulled a few others from her cart.

A knock at the door startled her, and she dropped the green bolt onto Nix, who wiggled and pounced around under the mossy puddle. The seamstress frowned, and Josephine quickly removed the cat.

"There's a gentleman to see you," the footman said.

Lucy thanked him and motioned to invite her guest in, her heart full of excitement. She had barely seen Lord Blackwell since his initial introduction to Alarik. She missed the daily walks and dinners and wanted to hear his thoughts on the castle and everything else on Orion. She checked her hair in the mirror. The braid pulled at the edges, and the gold-and-purple amethyst clasp holding it in place had fallen to the side. She looked frightful.

Instead of Lord Blackwell, Jasper's frame filled the door, and Lucy's heart sank.

"Oh, it's you," she said with a sigh. "Where have you been?"

He looked ready to murder, and Lucy was almost afraid for a moment. The seamstress discreetly moved to the sewing cart at the far side of the room and out of earshot.

"Lord Daye is having me followed. I haven't been able to get near you without someone noticing. There is a pile of people trailing you everywhere you go." He eyed her warily as he stepped over the pile of half-sewn dresses and sat down. He crossed one leg over the other, resting his heel on his knee and draping an arm over the back of the chaise.

"Yes, I was aware Lord Daye was having me followed. He fancies we're in love and have plans to run away together. It's a good thing he's unaware of your obsession with Lady Daye. But before any more dreary talk—because I do have news for you—what do you think?" Lucy set the black silk under her chin, then shifted back to the pinkish purple. "And don't give me a look. I've seen your shoes. It's perfectly acceptable to love all of this—not everything beautiful is corrupt. What about red?"

"Not red," Jasper said with a scowl, then stood and joined the seamstress at the cart. Pulling a lemon-yellow silk from the stack, he brought it over and held it up.

Lucy looked at herself, enjoying the sunny glow of the fabric.

It reminded her of the first gown Wynter had made for her.

"Will Lord Blackwell like it?" she asked absently. "I shouldn't care, but for unexplainable reasons, I want him to think I look pretty—no, not pretty. I want him to think I'm beautiful, stunning even. Am I stunning?"

Jasper's face remained blank, but the blade came out of his pocket and resumed its usual clicking. "Most people walk away from an encounter with you stunned to some degree, I'd say."

"I didn't mean in a shocking way—although…"

"You said you have news?" he asked impatiently.

Lucy didn't want to create undue optimism, but Jasper had been right—her staff at the castle trusted her and had talked freely with her.

"I've been asking around. You'll never guess what I uncovered, quite easily actually. Lady Daye was seen talking to Madame Helix on the night of the ball. It gets better. Their meeting happened right before Lady Cristelle and Ward had their falling out, which, as you know, was before Helix accused Wynter of murder."

Jasper took in the news and stood quietly for a moment, as if he was putting the pieces together.

He hadn't been on Orion, or even in the Hex-system, the night Lady Daye disappeared, but Lucy remembered it all like a bad dream. The ball itself had been splendid. Wynter had designed the most glorious dress for her to wear. Lady Cristelle had taken Ward out to the garden, where everyone expected she'd propose marriage. But when they returned, she was saying the most terrible things, as Lucy knew was the plan. She didn't approve of how Lady Cristelle had handled the whole situation, but Lady Cristelle would likely disapprove of the lambs—they both had their own way of dealing with the pressures of life as a lady.

Then the missing Madame Helix had barged into the ballroom and accused Wynter of murder. All of this had happened after Helix and Lady Daye were seen talking together. And no one knew where Madame Helix had been in the days leading up to the ball.

"From what you told me before, Madame Helix and Lady Daye did not get along. You're suggesting they were working together?"

Lucy shrugged. "They didn't like each other. My aunt always made it very clear that I was never to wear a Helix gown and never been seen in her company. But many people believe Lady Cristelle and I don't get along either. It's convenient to have an enemy around, especially when there's trouble. The best part is that Madame Helix wasn't sent to a factory to work. No one knows where she is, but it's rumoured that a friend of mine does, and of course I have a delightfully sneaky plan to contact him. Can you get this to Lord Blackwell? I haven't seen him either." Lucy scribbled a note and passed it to Jasper, who folded it and tucked it into his breast pocket.

Their meeting concluded, Lucy called the seamstress back over and made a few last notes; she made arrangements to pick up her new dress the following afternoon. It was hard to contain so much excitement. After finally uncovering information about Lady Daye, for the first time she felt there was a chance. A chance that her aunt could be found and life could go back to normal, whatever normal looked like.

Twenty-Five

Lucy wore a deep aqua-blue top that fell over one shoulder and dipped down her back like a waterfall. Josephine wove blue lilies and a small strand of sapphires into her hair.

She met up with Jasper first. He wore all black and was leaning against a wall with carved arches. He looked unnecessarily dangerous.

"You know people talk about you," Lucy said, walking up to him.

"You know people talk about you," he retorted.

"Of course they do, but not because they think they're going to be murdered in their sleep. There's different kinds of talk."

"Perhaps I like the way they talk." Jasper gave her a wicked grin.

Lord Blackwell approached from the other end of the hall. He was casually dressed and more relaxed. Being on land certainly made a difference to him. He glanced to where Lucy's arm was tucked over Jaspers. "I got your message last night. Where are we going?"

"Wynter's dress shop," Lucy answered.

"You don't need my opinion on every dress," Jasper said dryly, earning a look from Lord Blackwell.

"Lord Daye is being pesky and is having someone trail all of us. The staff have been fantastic, moving me around the castle without notice and distracting the men following you—but anyone could be assisting him. So we're all headed to Wynter's shop."

Before she could explain more, Zandra and two other women joined them, dressed similarly to Lucy. As they walked down the hall, a group of six and then another group of two joined them. Then the whole gathering spilled from the castle, down the courtyard, and into the village.

The spring festival was Lucy's favourite. Music poured into the streets and wound around every open booth. The sun shone down on canopies set out to shade the shoppers. The cool of winter had passed, and everything was in full bloom.

All the guilds, all the work. So much pride and talent went into each item. As the group made its way through the festival Lucy talked to everyone and bought items at each booth. She found a lace top for Josephine, and a bottle of perfume for one of the women in the kitchens who collected the little bottles. She bought chocolates and sweets and passed most of the packages to Lord Blackwell to carry.

"I thought we were supposed to be sneaky," Jasper stated, the joy of the afternoon doing little to warm up his cool attitude.

"Exactly. The two of you on my arm will draw unwanted attention. It's like sunshine surrounded by clouds."

After lunch, they lost more than half of their group and made their way to Wynter Canmore's shop. The front display was a bloom of spring colours: minty-green day dresses and patterned whites, creams, and light yellows.

Lucy walked in first and greeted Wynter's head seamstress. Lucy wished it was Wynter there to see her, but she was on the Obsidian and not likely to return soon. "Hello, Clair! Oh, it's so good to see you." A soft lace apron covered a bold black dress, and Clair enveloped Lucy in a tight hug.

There were baskets of mending and a row of four children working away, one woman teaching them.

"The next round of fashion designers, if any want to stay on," Clair said, introducing the girls, who all smiled at Lucy in quiet awe.

Lucy pulled a few new gowns from the racks. Jasper and Lord Blackwell took a seat on the overstuffed silver chairs and watched as Lucy came out with the first one on. It rumpled and ruffled in all the wrong places.

"How dreadfully unflattering. I wasn't planning to buy this one anyway, but I wanted to see it on. My gown for the ball is almost finished… fitting is going to take an extra few minutes. More than a few. It's going to be a while, so you two will just have to wait. Maybe Clair can find you something to drink."

Lucy slipped back into the dressing room as quick as lightning, slid out of the silver gown, and tossed it to Clair. She donned a black sweater and loose fitting pants.

She covered herself with a long cape and pulled the hood down low—something she wouldn't dare be seen in. Clair opened the back door for her, and Lucy slipped into the alleyway behind the shop.

It wouldn't do to have Jasper and Lord Blackwell following her. She needed to be seen out with them and remembered by those who saw her.

Three doors down, she came to a narrow door between two of the shops and knocked three times.

Twenty-Six

The knocks were answered by a guard with blond hair and a strong square jaw—someone Josephine would be immediately attracted to. Lucy made a mental note to mention him to her and then crossed the stone threshold. The narrow hallway felt snug; the overpowering pattern of lemons and plums that splattered the papered walls made her want to run until she reached the sitting rooms.

She had brought a bag of chocolates for the guards, who were always happy to see her. It wasn't much of a prison but more of a home in a row of closed-off houses. The front looked like any other.

Lucy walked into a well-furnished room. There were piles of books and notes scattered everywhere. Lab supplies cluttered the couches. Empty haze bottles sprinkled the floor, and half-drunk bottles lined the wall. Lucy stepped around the broken glass and shook off a piece of red seal-wax that stuck to her shoe. She hated seeing him like this.

"Dr Moss?" Lucy called into the mess. She'd visited him frequently those first few months, before she was summoned to

Valtine. She wondered what he'd been up to in the long months she was gone and if he'd missed her at all—probably not.

The guilds didn't know what to do with Dr Moss. They couldn't prove anything against him, and he was working with some powerful people granting Wynter Canmore, the dressmaker, her shop and safety on the Obsidian. In exchange for these favours, Dr Moss offered his assistance—at least that's what she'd overheard. Wynter still believed Captain Ward had purchased her freedom, but since that relationship was precariously romantic, Lucy kept the bit about Dr Moss's involvement to herself.

Dr Moss came out of a side room, holding a datapad. Despite the state of his room, he looked very well put together. He was devilishly handsome. Muscled arms stretched the black rolled-up sleeves. He looked like he could crush her in an instant, but growing up with her father had been much the same.

"Wynter wanted me to give this to you the next time I saw you—although it's old news, and contains nothing I didn't already know." She handed him the half-crumpled letter. He tucked it into his pocket as if it wasn't important, but he would read every word the moment she left.

Lucy toed another bit of broken glass with her boot. "You're breaking things?" She stepped past the covered chairs and hoisted herself up onto a clean counter. Wincing as her back pulled, Lucy could feel where the burns still hadn't fully healed.

"You haven't seen me in a dozen moon cycles, and you want to talk about my drinking?"

"I was talking about breaking things. Do you want to talk about your drinking?" Lucy asked.

"No."

"Should you talk about your drinking?"

He scowled at her. She resisted the urge to reach out and push on one of the muscled arms to see if they were as hard as they looked.

"Actually, I'm here to talk about my aunt. But someone needs to remind you it's not a good idea. You're far too intelligent to be drowning it all away."

He stopped, crossed his arms over his chest, and looked her over from head to toe. She swung her foot back and forth, waiting, and gave him an equally intense once-over. He was an incredibly handsome man.

"What are you wearing?" he asked, losing the first battle.

"Do you like it?"

"No, it's terrible." He opened a lower cupboard and pulled out a brass coffee pot and two cups, thumping them down loudly enough for a guard to poke his head in and check on Lucy. She waved him off.

"Well, since you're clearly not in the mood to hand out compliments, perhaps I won't show you what's in my bag," Lucy pouted.

Dr Moss folded his arms across his chest again. "You want a compliment on your outfit in exchange for giving me something I didn't ask for?"

"Well, a girl can dream." Lucy untied her bag and shuddered, then pulled out the black netted corset.

Immediately intrigued, Dr Moss took it from her.

"Jasper said you might be interested. Of course, he didn't

realize he'd even mentioned your name. I'm very good at pretending I'm not listening."

Dr Moss mumbled something about incompetent men. Laying it flat, he connected it to a datapad. Its black netting rippled under the lights.

"It's not the only reason I'm here. I'm trying to find Lady Daye—there's a whole situation with a proposal and me not wanting to live like a lady on Valtine—all horribly boring. You know something about Idex and security and I thought you could find someone for me."

Ignoring her, Dr Moss cleared a space and set two screens side-by-side, comparing the information.

"The output on this is completely fried and would have caused significant pain. You wore this?" Dr Moss asked.

Lucy nodded and wondered if it had been worth it. She was still engaged to Lord Blackwell, and Lord Daye still had more control than she cared to admit, even under her father's roof.

"I'll locate someone for you if you show me your burns." The look in his eyes nearly floored her. Compassion coming from Dr Moss had a devastating effect.

Lucy lifted the side of her sweater to show one of the burn lines that curled up her ribs. It hadn't healed the way a burn should. She remembered being burned as a child—it had hurt, but she'd healed quickly enough and had only a light scar to show for it. These had stopped hurting, aside from an occasional twinge, but the deep-crimson marks remained.

"Why do they look like this?" Lucy asked.

"It was set to your Idex. This kind of tech is dangerous and experimental at best. You must have made someone desperate to control you." Dr Moss rummaged through his cupboards until he found a little grey jar. He unscrewed the lid, then added something white, a few drops of a dark-blue liquid, and finally something with a silver shine.

"I brought a few lambs into a ball. Lord Daye decided I needed some reeducation."

"Foolish man—he was clearly in over his head."

"Yes, but so am I." Lucy swallowed a lump. The weight of the scars and the depth of the trouble she was in weighed too heavily. "I'm engaged to Lord Blackwell, and unless I find Madame Helix, who will tell me what happened to Lady Daye, I might have to marry a Valtine lord. Everyone believed Madame Helix was sent into forced factory labour, except we don't have that on Orion, and we know she hasn't left the planet."

"That's a lot of information all at once."

"I figured you'd be able to keep up."

He came close, leaned on the counter, and flexed his jaw. His proximity was a weak attempt to intimidate her before whatever he would say next.

"That doesn't work on me," Lucy said, taking the small jar from his hand.

"Your aunt has been missing for over a year. Either she is somewhere safe and doesn't want to be found—or she's dead."

"Or in danger. Jasper thinks it's danger," Lucy added. "He found something before coming to Valtine and only hints at it. His story doesn't add up, which means there has to be more to it. I am worried about him. Unlike you, he doesn't drink. He just flicks his knife and looks dangerously at everyone. And don't pretend Jasper is a stranger to you—you didn't even flinch when I mentioned his name earlier.”

“Jasper doesn’t need your pity or protection.”

“And I don’t need yours—although a compliment would be nice. So perhaps you can locate Madame Helix for me?”

Dr Moss opened a drawer at the bottom of a cupboard. It was so thin it could easily have been missed. He took out a third datapad and within minutes had a location for Madame Helix, but hesitated handing it over.

“Women like you are the reason men like me drink,”

“We both know the opposite is true,” Lucy said saucily.

“You mistake my meaning. It is not having you in our lives, but what is left when you are gone. I do not want to put you in danger.”

The momentary sweetness set her back again.

“Don’t worry, Jasper is with me—” Lucy tried the name again, wondering if Dr Moss would tell her how they were connected.

He scrawled something on a piece of paper, folded it, and handed it to her.

“Give this to Jasper. And no, I will not explain how I know him.”

She tucked the slip of paper into her pocket.

“He’s dangerous,” Dr Moss warned, with the same tone Lord Daye had used. Perhaps he assumed an emotional attachment on her part. It was wild to her that so many assumed she would give away her heart that easily.

“Don’t worry, I’m not interested. You, on the other hand...” she raised a brow, hoping to throw him off. He handed her a fourth datapad, much smaller than the others.

“Here are the directions. There are no markings, and it’s off the path, but you'll see it. Next time, bring me some of those chocolates," he growled.

Lucy hopped off the counter, took the datapad, and surprised him with a kiss on the cheek. "You cannot save the world if you cannot take care of yourself," she said, with a last look at the bottles. She passed him a small bag of chocolates from her bag.

Lucy left Dr Moss, wondering if he would enjoy having a cat as a pet. Probably not. She slipped back down the alley and into Wynter's shop. Passing the cape to the waiting Clair, she emerged breathless from the dressing room.

"No matter what we tried, the dress does not fit. I'm just going to come back again later," Lucy announced to the room.

Jasper had a stack of bolts lined up as if he were putting in an order for himself. Lord Blackwell was talking to a seamstress who was sitting on the edge of his chair, laughing easily with her. The slightest pang of jealousy ran through her, and she wondered why he didn't try harder to break the engagement. He was a very eligible lord. He was kind and delightful to be around. Any lady would surely make an offer of marriage to him—at least any lady who wanted to marry.

At her request, they abandoned their distractions and left the shop together. A large white trolley with silver trim and navy seats pulled up. They climbed on, thankful to rest for the remainder of the journey back to the castle. Lucy wanted to climb in beside Lord Blackwell, who put his arm on the back of the bench. She was sure she'd fit perfectly nudged up beside him. Instead, she climbed up beside Jasper. She took the folded note out of her dress pocket and passed it to him.

"Dr Moss wanted me to give this to you."

"You talked to Dr Moss?" Jasper whispered.

"I see him all the time. Well, I did for those few months before leaving for Valtine. I have the location for Madame Helix." Lucy enjoyed the momentary shock. "I imagine he's lonely. Besides, he might be twice my age, but even I can appreciate seeing a man that good-looking from time to time."

Twenty-Seven

Lord Blackwell was quick to agree to the mission to find Madame Helix. With less than four weeks until the wedding, Alarik approved of some of the younger lords and ladies taking some time away from the capital to celebrate the upcoming event, which gave Lucy the perfect cover.

The lies stuck like glue in Lucy's heart, but any time she tried to get a moment alone with Alarik, he was called away.

Jasper didn't join them, but informed them that he was going to follow another mysterious lead. At one point, he'd started explaining himself, then stopped mid-sentence and walked away as if he realized they didn't require an explanation.

The group travelling to the island destination was far from small. Lucy had a dozen friends accompanying her—and she did her best to remember all of their names. It was a happy group, ready to enjoy some sun and relaxation. Most importantly, Madame Helix could be found not far from their destination.

A plum sunset melted into the night as the shuttle carried

them to the far side of the planet.

Lucy looked out the window and tapped her fingers on the armrest. The seat beside her was piled with trunks and bags that didn't fit in the storage compartments. She had to make it look like she was operating as normally as possible and not on a mission to find information—to find Madame Helix.

No one would believe she'd actually fallen for Lord Blackwell and not brought at least thirty gowns with her.

Lucy looked down as they descended.

The shore glistened in the moonlight. A walkway on the water glowed. Lights dangled down the pier and connected to the village below.

Large white cottages clustered together along the long beach.

Lucy yawned as the shuttle landed. She grabbed her pink travelling bag, leaving the rest for the staff to retrieve, and accepted Lord Blackwell's offered arm. They disembarked and walked along the wooden plank walkway to the waiting trolleys which took them to their cottages.

Despite their late hour, a dinner had been prepared and set between the cottages. A round tent with sides pulled back held a dozen tables. Flowers and shells decorated them, and twinkling lights hung suspended between the poles. She ordered a soft orange twist with spirals of citrus peels.

Lucy talked and laughed easily through the dinner.

Lord Blackwell said little and leaned back in his chair, enjoying the conversation around him. She had rarely seen him so relaxed—wearing informal attire, at informal events. His manner looked almost inviting. Lucy squashed the desire, recognizing her growing attachment. She knew these feelings, even though she'd never experienced them herself—and she could not, would not, fall for a Valtine lord, especially one her uncle wanted her to marry.

When the final dishes had been served and consumed, the music started.

Lucy turned to Lord Blackwell. She'd never danced with him, not properly, not freely.

She blushed. He was only there to help her and was not obligated to dance with her. But he stood, pushing the chair back.

Lucy twirled under the stars, and he guided her quickly through the large group of dancers. Lord Blackwell's dancing skills lacked nothing.

When the music changed, she didn't make a move to switch partners, and neither did he. The swing of the song pulled them closer as he slowly turned her. His eyes held hers, and a hint of a dimple appeared as he half smiled. Holding her upper back, he dipped her low, then pulled her back up into his arms. His hand rested high on the back of her neck, fingers entwined in the curls of her hair.

Lucy stopped, suspended under the stars. Their quest was almost forgotten, as was the fact that he was a Valtine lord.

When the music stopped, Lord Trife stepped up beside them and abruptly took her hand for the next dance. Lord Blackwell was immediately engaged with another lady.

It wasn't jealousy she felt, but it was hard to not want to abandon her new partner and run across the dance floor, demanding Lord Blackwell's undivided attention. He smiled for the other lady too, and she couldn't help but wonder if this was the kind of feeling that caused others to behave so poorly.

After three more dances, she was ready to retire for the evening; they had a full day of pretending and sneaking coming up.

Lucy yawned and begged her leave as the music continued playing from the centre of the dance floor and floated into the night.

Before she had gone far, Lord Blackwell was at her side, taking her arm to escort her back. A flutter of flames filled her stomach, and her heart beat fast. It was a kind and gentlemanly thing to do, and she knew she shouldn't read too much into it. But no one would see them. This wasn't part of the charade. He said nothing but led her down the moonlit path.

She yawned again and leaned into him a little. He slowed his steps.

"What are you thinking?" he asked, breaking the silence.

"I bet you never expected you'd have to ask me," Lucy nudged him and he chuckled. "I was thinking how wonderful it would be if we were really celebrating our upcoming marriage, and all of this was real."

They had reached Lucy's cottage. Lord Blackwell stiffened and turned to face her, concerned etched between his brows.

"Of course it's not, and I don't want it to be," Lucy bumbled, mortified that she'd said it out loud. This was worse than the comments about kissing. "It's just that if it was, it would have been perfect. You played the part of enamoured fiancé very well."

"It's been my honour," he said gallantly, but the look he gave her made her wonder if he wished it was over already. But of course he did, and she should too. She had no intentions of marrying him. He was quiet and reserved and so perfectly boring, and Lucy knew she would do nothing but bring shame and embarrassment and who knows what else to his family. Of course he wouldn't ever be interested in her. Why did she care so much? Her thoughts darted around her feelings like a rabbit, and she struggled to say anything else.

What was she waiting for? For him to declare his love for her? What a ridiculous notion.

Josephine opened the door behind her, and Lucy hesitated again.

Lord Blackwell bowed slightly, then left her at the door.

Lucy watched him go, keeping one foot inside the door where Josephine sorted piles of dresses that had exploded from the trunks. She saw him walk casually toward his own cottage, stop for a moment to look up at the moon and stars, and then turn to look back at her. Their eyes locked. He tilted his head in acknowledgment, then disappeared inside.

Lucy closed the door, overwhelmed by the desire to run back outside and knock on Lord Blackwell's door. But what would she say? *Thank you?* Surely the whole thing had gone far beyond misplaced responsibility. A tightness and dread filled her. They were only saying good night. She would see him first thing in the morning.

But someday, and someday soon, she would have to say goodbye forever. The engagement was fake, and once everything worked out, he would leave and return to his quiet life—a life she was not part of. The squeeze in her chest tightened—if saying good night hurt like this, what would saying goodbye feel like?

"Are you alright?" Josephine asked. "Did we forget

something?"

Lucy turned on her heel to survey the pile of dresses, shaking off the dread.

"I can't imagine forgetting anything we would need. I'm alright. Sometimes there is an unexplainable ache in my chest." Lucy paused and picked up a soft cream dress with lavender lace. She tossed it over a chair, then picked up another dress and held it to her chest. "I can sense something… under my skin. Like there's something I'm missing. I think I'm lonely. That's it—I'm just lonely, and that's not a reason to have all sorts of feelings."

"Are you having feelings? For Lord Blackwell?"

"No—of course not," Lucy said hurriedly. She undressed and put on a white evening gown. The open windows welcomed in a salty breeze. Lucy snuggled under the sage-green blanket and stared up at the ceiling. Intricate iron work made a crisscross pattern of flowers and wild birds. It wasn't perfect, but it was earthy and felt like home.

She was having more than feelings for Lord Blackwell. Slowly and steadily, the fantasy born in the darkness of the library had followed her through the stars and stalked her heart. Lucy was always keenly aware of her feelings and acted accordingly, and she knew this one. She was dangerously close to love.

When she awoke, she dressed in a lemon-yellow dress that flared out just above her knee. A single strap decked with artificial pink and white orchids curved around her neck and under her pinned-up hair.

They met for breakfast on a dock that detached and floated

out on the water. Lord Blackwell was wearing fashionably loose white pants. The short sleeves of his top highlighted well-muscled arms. The wind caught his hair and tousled it. Like the night before, he looked relaxed. The hollow pain came back—like it was all going to disappear at any moment. Like he was going to disappear. She would be left standing on the beach. Like when her aunt left after the ball, and Lady Cristelle left on a grand adventure, and Wynter left... well, that one made sense.

Lucy didn't like the sad thoughts. She brushed them off as she joined him at the table.

The point of the trip was twofold, and if anyone was to believe they were a true couple, they had to visit with other guests. Lucy usually didn't mind—Lord Blackwell was surprisingly nice to talk to, as she'd learned on the Aurora, and now that he was on land and relaxed, he was even more pleasant to be around. But at this breakfast, they were seated with Lady Vance and her husband. The woman was at least twenty years older than Lucy and talked endlessly about her collection of rare artifacts. It wasn't the collection itself that was so boring, but the way in which Lady Vance detailed how she'd acquired each piece by highlighting their value.

"I wonder how someone decides that an object has a certain value—who gets to make that decision? If something is no longer useful, what makes it valuable?" Lucy asked as she leaned her spoon upright against her knife and fork, trying to make them stand on their own. The cutlery tower clattered onto the table, and Lucy looked up. Everyone was uncomfortably silent for a moment.

Lord Vance scrunched his nose, and Lady Vance stirred her

tea aggressively, glaring at Lord Blackwell as if the social misstep were his fault. Lucy felt a pang of guilt; she had no intention of changing who she was, but the blunder reflected poorly on him. She didn't want to apologize, but neither did she want Lord Blackwell to feel uncomfortable. She stole a glance in his direction and was surprised that he didn't look the least bit upset. He passed over his discarded knife and spoon, adding to Lucy's building materials, then leaned back in his chair with a cup of steaming coffee in hand. Lucy returned to her build, and after a moment, Lady Vance continued to talk but spoke of her seashell collection instead.

When the final plates had been served and consumed, Lord Blackwell suggested a private ride inland. It was part of the plan, but Lucy was excited to be heading out alone with him.

She sprinted back to her cottage, where Josephine helped her change three times before deciding on smart pants and a light flowered top. Lord Blackwell waited patiently for her. She climbed onto the back of the speeder, seated behind him with her arms wrapped around his waist.

They followed Dr Moss's directions and took the speeder inland, travelling a road that wound through tropical trees and dense vegetation. It narrowed and widened again at odd angles.

The wind whipped around them, catching Lucy's blond curls and sending them flying. When they stopped, she felt very much like a lion after a tornado and tried detangling them with her fingers.

Lord Blackwell got off the bike, helped her down, and then stood in front of her. He ran his fingers through her hair, gently smoothing the worst of the knots, then turned her, pulled it all back, and repinned it. Lucy closed her eyes for a minute, taking in the sweetness of his touch. It was simple, helpful, and so incredibly wonderful. If she could freeze this moment and hold it forever, she would. But they were standing in front of the large home where Madame Helix was supposed to be hiding.

Lucy strode up the steps, calming her nerves with a friendly smile, and rang the bell.

No one answered.

Social engagements were usually preplanned. She rang again, counted to ten, then rang once more. When she raised her hand after counting to ten again, Lord Blackwell grabbed it midair to stop her.

Noise from inside the house was decidedly slow despite Lucy's continuous rings. An elderly woman—not Helix—answered the door, frowning. Her grey hair was pulled back in a tidy bun. Her cheeks were too big and her nose too small. Perhaps if she'd smiled, she would have had a kindly face. But the woman did not smile.

"On the back porch," she snapped and slammed the door in their faces.

Twenty-Eight

Black iron rails locked clear panes of glass in place, highlighting the sheer drop off the side of the porch. Lucy led the way down the side of the house and around the back.

Helix sat on a long chaise, facing a cliff that looked into a ravine of trees and sharp rocks. Her hands were busy stitching a blanket covered with little flowers. It was pretty and simple and not at all Helix.

"Madame Helix. Hello," Lucy called out, crossing the veranda. Lucy was almost in front of her before she looked up.

"It took you long enough to show up. And here I thought you'd never come," Helix said. The needle pulled a yellow string in long loops, finishing another daisy. "Lord Blackwell, nice to see you."

He bowed gracefully over her hand and complimented her stitching.

"I get the regular news, as you see, but I'm rare for company. No one is supposed to know I'm here, of course. Well, why don't you come in?" Helix tossed the white linen onto the porch as if it were a bit of rubbish and not a carefully stitched pattern. Her mulberry dress caught under a bit of the blanket. She tugged it, sending an embroidered corner through one of the floorboard cracks. Then she ushered them into the large cottage.

The elderly woman who'd first answered the door appeared again. A tray with cakes and cookies was already set out. Helix didn't acknowledge the woman as she turned and left the sitting room.

"I actually expected you much sooner. Although that dreadful man you call an uncle kept you longer on Valtine than he should have. Well, time cannot be undone."

Lucy gaped at her. How could she possibly have expected Lucy there sooner?

Lucy sat on the overstuffed, itchy lounge chair and glanced around the room. The mantel above the fireplace was cluttered with vases, pins, towers of ribbons, and tiny ceramic mice. Between two mice, she recognized the elaborate hair pieces her aunt had worn. Lucy stood, staring at the very one she'd seen Lady Daye wear to the ball.

"Is she here? Is Aunt Daye here?" Lucy exclaimed, ready to search the entire place.

The elderly lady came running in at her aunt's name and glared at Lucy.

"Of course not—sit down, foolish girl," Madame Helix growled.

Waiting until the elderly woman was out of earshot, Lucy wondered if she was some sort of guard. Either way, Helix clearly didn't want her overhearing their conversation.

"I thought this was her hairpiece." Lucy felt foolish. Of course, there might be similar ones all over the hex-system.

Helix turned her focus to Lord Blackwell. "I heard the two of you are getting married? When?"

"Lord Daye set a date less than four weeks from now," Lord Blackwell said, which was the truth. The date had been set. He leaned back and looked irritatingly calm.

"Tell me everything of Valtine," Helix demanded.

Lucy looked around and noticed the various crafts. Spun lace covered every table. The chair she was sitting on was carefully detailed in bead work. Sharp bobbles poked into her when she sat on it. The curtains were floor length and billowy, covered with odd designs.

She took pity on the woman in front of her.

Helix looked bored, and Lucy could at least sympathize.

Lucy played along and regaled her with tales of all the balls she had hosted. She was careful not to mention the dresses Wynter had designed for her. When Helix asked how they'd come to agree to the match, Lucy mentioned the lambs, then blushed—knowing it was corsets and not lambs that had brought them together.

"My goodness, Lord Daye must be desperate to get you married. It makes perfect sense that he chose Lord Blackwell—just the type to make you behave."

Lucy straightened her back and lifted her chin at the insinuation.

"Well, you've appeased me. And so I will give you what you are looking for, but first I want something in return."

"I'm not sure what I can give you—" And Lucy wasn't sure what she was looking for other than Lady Daye.

Helix held up a hand.

"When you marry Lord Blackwell, I want to design your

dress. And I promise it will be horrible." She paused for effect. Lucy indulged, moving to the edge of the couch and letting a shocked expression play across her face. Lord Blackwell was watching her closely. And Helix was looking between the two of them, interested in the moment. "I want you to tell everyone that Wynter Canmore designed it. You are not to alter it in any way, and you must wear it for the duration of the ceremony. I want a contract in writing."

Helix yelled for the elderly woman, who materialized immediately with a datapad and contract. Lucy was certain she'd been able to overhear everything they said. "Go outside and talk it over while I order tea."

Lord Blackwell rose from his seat and went outside, the soft screen magnets closing behind him.

Lucy followed him out onto the veranda, where he stood at the railing, looking down the sharp ravine.

Perfectly rounded thistle bushes grew in a tidy row around the trees. Perhaps there was a purpose behind them—or perhaps Helix just liked them.

"This might work in our favour. We're only a month away from the wedding, and we still need a plan to end our engagement. If I never find my aunt—you can refuse to marry me because I'm wearing a dreadful dress."

"This has gone on too long. You're home, you're safe. We can end this now—we should end this now. You would walk all the way down an aisle to be rejected, just to find your aunt?" he asked, and Lucy wondered what it would feel like to walk down a long aisle toward him, ready to make a vow.

"It's a small price to pay, and it likely won't be the last. I'm not too worried about it—I look fantastic no matter what I'm wearing."

The hot muggy air suspended the moment. Lucy sighed and leaned up on her toes and over the railing, where she spied tiny flowers growing between the thistles.

"What do you want to do?" he asked.

I want to marry you—the thought materialized unbidden into Lucy's mind. She swallowed a lump.

Lucy wondered what he was thinking. Would he be willing to go all the way down an aisle with her just to find her aunt?

The rattling of Helix and a tea tray clamoured from inside.

"I want to find Lady Daye. I need to help Jasper," she whispered instead. "And you won't be marrying me, so there's no chance of me ruining Wynter's reputation as a dressmaker."

Lord Blackwell took a step back and folded his arms. "No, no risk of that."

"If she doesn't have anything useful for me, we'll end this as soon as we're back at the castle. If she does, well, we still need to end it but maybe just a bit later. And I promise—you won't be forced to see me in a hideous gown." Lucy turned and leaned her elbows on the railing. This was all getting to be too much.

"I would hate to have to see you wearing something ugly. If you're sure you want to make a deal with her, then I'm with you." He pushed off and reentered the house.

How terrible could the dress be?

Twenty-Nine

Helix made a grand show of pouring tea and handing the small cup to Lord Blackwell. He was polite and relaxed—all the concern from only moments before wiped from his face.

"I'll do it, but I want to know why," Lucy said, reaching for a teacup. Helix slapped her hand. Lucy pulled it back and frowned at the sting.

"Not that one," Helix said, then passed her the teacup beside it. "Revenge can be enjoyable—pleasant even. Wynter and I could have worked something out, after I took her in, cared for her, taught her everything she knew—shielded her from the outside world. Wynter may have come up with the elaborate gowns, but I stitched every other dress those women wore. We never would have sold anything if it wasn't for me putting dresses on the racks. She has incredible talent, but I taught her what to do with it. After everything I did for her, she could have at least talked to me about it. But she let her silly captain turn her head, and she ended up with everything. A shop on Orion and my shop on the Obsidian. And I'm stuck here."

Lucy thought back to shoe shopping with Wynter, and of the truth of what Helix had done. She hadn't paid Wynter for a single dress she'd sewn for her. There was also Wynter's compelling accusation that Helix had killed. More than once. It didn't seem necessary to point that out to her. Someone who could commit such atrocities wouldn't forget them easily—they just didn't care.

"I accept," Lucy said. It felt wrong making a deal with the woman, but it wasn't a real contract. It was a fake wedding, after all.

Madame Helix grabbed a datapad from a shelf. Turning it on, she reviewed the information on the screen.

It was a pre prepared, ironclad, detailed contract, and she passed it to Lord Blackwell. She motioned for Lucy to stand and grabbed a long measuring tape from behind a cushion. Pulling Lucy's arms up, Helix ran the tape from her wrist to her shoulder as Lucy tried to look over and see the document.

Every detail of the dress was outlined. It had been written months ago. The only thing missing was Lord Blackwell's name. If she didn't marry Lord Blackwell, then the contract would stand no matter who it was.

"Are you sure this is what you want? This is official. There will be no going back on it," Lord Blackwell said, giving her one more chance to back out.

"Of course." Lucy took it out of his hands and signed it, tossing it onto the chair and straightening to finish the measurements.

Helix grinned like an evil wasp. She called in the elderly woman, who had a datapad of her own. The contract was uploaded.

At least if Lord Daye discovered Lucy's visit to Helix, she'd have an excuse for being there. Wedding dresses.

Helix scribbled notes as she worked and didn't waste any time telling her story—with as much subtle flare as she'd used to sell her gowns.

"Lady Daye lived here for three months after the ball." Helix took a bolt of brown fabric from a long cupboard and eyed Lucy over the edge, letting the news settle in.

Lady Daye had not disappeared right away.

Months. Lucy had remained on Orion for those months. She'd helped Wynter set up her shop. Her aunt had been on the other side of the planet, and hadn't said anything to her. Didn't seek her out to explain. Nothing. She hadn't even said goodbye.

"It was impossible to leave the planet, and so she came to the one person who had a gift for hiding people in plain sight."

Lucy couldn't picture her aunt staying in this cottage with no parties to plan and nothing to do. She wondered if any of the decorations were her creations. No one had even bothered to look here. There was obviously bad blood between Madame Helix and Lady Daye.

"I wondered if you didn't hate each other as much as you pretended to—but why would my aunt come here?"

"Hated? Well, no. We've had our moments. The problem with young people these days is that they think they are the only ones with lives. You simply stumbled into a story much older than you are. As did Wynter. Lady Daye and I were great friends when we were younger, almost sisters. We met on Orion when we were girls, close to here. Lady Daye had just lost her parents, and her brother had taken her away from

Valtine to grieve. We got a little wrapped up in a radical group —we were going to save the hex-system."

Helix rolled her eyes at her own comment, slung the measuring tape around her shoulder, and picked up her cup of tea, taking a slow sip before continuing.

"We fell in love with the same man. He was only a few years older than our young sixteen, but he seemed so much older at the time. We were too young and should never have been allowed into such a dangerous organization. Henris was the worst. He talked about doing the right thing, but when the time came, he chose to protect his own life instead of getting the help needed to save Domo. It was all covered up anyway, so it's not like he was at risk."

"How did they cover up something so huge?" Lucy asked. Wynter and Lady Cristelle had both told her varying stories about the medical lab in the mountains. A rescue attempt failed when an explosion levelled the compound.

"Lady Daye agreed to marry Lord Daye within three years, and he took care of the rest. We promised never to speak to each other again, and I found a position on the Obsidian. When Wynter came to me, I saw it as a moment to take my revenge and clean up the mess left behind. Something I'd not been able to do as a young girl. "

"If you and my aunt were friends, then why did she want me to stay away from you?"

"She thought you'd connect the dots quickly—she clearly overestimated you. It took much too long for you to get here, and you seem to know nothing of this."

"I was stuck on Valtine," Lucy defended herself, then realized Helix didn't actually care.

"Lady Daye knew you'd want to be friends with Wynter and couldn't take that risk. Not with Captain Ward in charge of the Obsidian. He really has no idea how many secrets are on board—and he still sails around with Rane like he's a fatherly sort." Helix sniffed again, as if she were above them all. "There's a reason the Obsidian was never tied to land. Anyway, those aren't my stories to tell. When Henris contacted me about Wynter and finding her a place on the Obsidian, I agreed, but not for his sake. He deserved to die."

Madame Helix jumped from one scattered story to the next, and Lucy scrambled to keep up as the past blended with the present. And under it all, Lucy wondered what kind of wedding dress she would create.

Lucy looked at the clock on the wall. The tea cooled to undrinkable. They'd been sitting and talking for well over two hours, and Lucy wondered if she'd signed the contract for nothing.

"Three months she spent here hiding until Lord Daye requested you return to Valtine. Lady Daye assumed he hadn't found a trace of her. I don't think he was looking very hard. Either way, she secured passage to the Drop."

Helix paused for effect.

Lucy had a clue—she knew where her aunt had been and where she went next, but to the Drop? This thread of information was hardly worth a wedding dress.

"The Drop is the Delver Riven Observation Pod, an abandoned moon satellite about an eight-hour shuttle ride away. It's one of the oldest ruins in the hex-system, so there's constant talk of its preservation or dismantling, but no one can decide and so it sits empty. I snuck there once as a teenager.

The Drop is spooky," Lucy explained to Lord Blackwell.

"Is this all you have for us? Hardly a fair trade for a wedding gown. There's not much information to go on," Lord Blackwell said.

"Oh no, I'd give you that information for free. I miss telling a good story. Lucy, dear—take my advice and stop looking for your aunt. She left for a reason, and things might not be playing out as she initially planned. But she wanted me to give you this, and trust me, this is worth so much more than a dress contract." Helix nodded to the elderly woman who had materialized in the doorway.

Lord Blackwell straightened.

Madame Helix held up a small silver case.

"I hate to be the one to tell you, Lucy, but there might be alternative reasons for your Lord Blackwell agreeing to marry you—he's practically salivating over this. I would bet everything he didn't expect to find this here."

<h1 style="text-align:center">Thirty</h1>

Lucy looked at Lord Blackwell, who swallowed and stared at the box. She knew he had a reason for coming to Orion; he'd had a reason for befriending Lord Daye and spending all that time together. He'd never lied about keeping information from her, and whatever this was, it looked important. It made sense —it seemed this was the last little missing bit he had told her about without actually saying so. This was why he'd followed her to Orion, and Helix was right: By the look on his face, he had not expected her to have the box.

"Well, are you going to take it? You paid dearly for it." Helix held up the datapad containing the contract for her wedding dress—for the wedding that would never happen.

Lucy took the silver chest and ran her hand across the cool metal. A simple crest was stamped on the front, and the crest matched her knife. It was his family's security box, but it was being given to her, not Lord Blackwell.

"She left it for you—to secure your future however you wanted to. I got what I needed from it and so did she. I would have burned this house to the ground before letting anyone else touch it—thankfully, no one tried. I suggest you guard it well, something I'm sure Lord Blackwell will help with." She unceremoniously got up and marched out of the house, returning to the porch without so much as a goodbye.

They exited out the front and walked down the path lined with thorns and flowers. She waited in vain for Lord Blackwell to say something. She handed him the box, and he placed it in the carrying bag on the speeder. She half expected him to disappear with it and leave her standing alone.

But he waited for her to climb onto the seat behind him. On the way to find Helix, Lucy had only thought of the adventure and the clues they were following. Now all she could think about was the man in front of her. She wrapped her arms around him and held on as they sped away. He'd befriended her uncle to locate that box—was his friendship with her any different? She'd always sensed there was something keeping him from getting too close. Was this it?

The rocks and trees flying past became a blur, like Lucy's thoughts as they sped and melded in a moving flash of memory.

When they reached the beach, Lucy couldn't take anymore. She squeezed Lord Blackwell tight a few times until he stopped, allowing her to dismount.

The sun was setting over the water, and it sank rapidly as she walked the long wooden pier. Faint lights blinked in the darkness where the stars met the ocean. She took her shoes off and dipped her toes in the water. Lord Blackwell followed, then sat down beside her.

"Are you going to tell me what the box is? Are you allowed to tell me?" Lucy asked, trying to stay calm as she swirled the water that barely reached up to her toes.

"I'm sorry, Lucy, if I'd ever imagined it would end up in your hands, I would have said something sooner. My grandfather created the box, along with dozens like it. When I befriended Lord Daye, I was trying to locate it. As I told you before, Lady Daye had asked questions about a security box, but nothing I shared was exceptionally secret. She already knew where it was located—and knew of its contents. What I didn't know was that she had a way to get it, which is something I still can't figure out. It was hidden in a desk. No one was able to get near it without alarms going off. Even the cleaning staff were carefully monitored, as well as anyone allowed to have access to it."

Lucy wondered if she should tell Lord Blackwell about Wynter and her lack of Idex. There were rumours, but the fewer people who knew about it, the safer it was for her.

"Does Lord Daye know the box was missing?" Lucy asked instead.

"If he did he would have come to Orion a lot sooner. He might have found out since arriving, though."

"How did you know it was missing?"

"I would tell you if I was at liberty to," Lord Blackwell said. Lucy didn't press the matter, it felt wrong to ask him to betray his confidence.

It was getting late. Their trip to the island had given Lord Blackwell what he was looking for, and they had a lead for Jasper. Soon both men would have what they wanted, and she'd be alone again. She knew they had to make the next move, but instead she wanted to stay sitting beside Lord Blackwell and not have to face the next thing.

"We should head back and plan to go to the Drop," Lucy said, wondering if he felt the same.

"You're thinking of going to the Drop to look for her?" he asked. His leg shifted, and she brushed her knee against his causing a flutter.

"I know it's a long shot; for all we know she's buried under Helix's cottage. But it's not dangerous or anything, and I need to help Jasper."

"Right. Jasper will want to know what we found," Lord Blackwell said a little coolly.

"Don't worry, I won't tell him about the box you recovered. I'm not even sure I want to know what's in it." Lucy tried to assure him, but for some reason, the distance between them grew… like stars in the sky that appeared so close together but were infinitely far apart. Something had shifted, changed.

He stood, signalling an end to their time on the pier. She reluctantly got up as well. The stars twinkled above, and the cool air made her shiver. He took off his jacket, and she knew he was going to wrap it around her shoulders.

She didn't want the kind gesture—she wasn't ready for him to walk her home and end everything.

Instead of taking the jacket, she shrugged out of her overdress, peeled off her stockings, and dove into the water.

Coming up, she gasped, then floated on her back, the black, inky water chilling her. The stars shone above her, and she felt the stillness of the sea commanding her to just breathe.

Everything rushed through her in a long, tangled web. Her aunt had left—and had not gone far. For months, she'd waited until it was safe to slip away. It wasn't impulsive. It was planned. She must have known Lucy would be forced to take her place and the turmoil that would cause.

She lay flat, moving her hands and feet as little as possible to stay afloat. Still and small, yet part of something so vast. She let the worries slink from her thoughts into her hair and out into the water, down through her fingers and toes.

Lord Blackwell knew Lady Daye had taken the silver box and he was charged with retrieving it before Lord Daye found out. Now that he had it, his interest in her felt different. Jasper was desperate to find Lady Daye but also was likely unaware of the missing box. Helix was going to design a wedding dress for a fake wedding. And when it was all over, she would be alone again.

Tears slipped from her eyes and mixed with the seawater.

When the cold had nearly numbed her through, she let her toes reach down to the sand under the waves and pushed toward the ladder. She couldn't see him at first, but then the moon illuminated his figure. Her dress was draped elegantly over one arm. He held open his jacket, which she readily climbed into, pulling the collar up to her chin and shivering.

"Aren't you going to tell me I'm foolish?" Lucy asked, starting the long, cold walk back.

"No—but you might have waited until we were closer to the cottages."

Lucy agreed as the chill made her shiver. They walked in silence, and for once, she didn't sense the need to fill the void. Her heart ached—torn, knowing she carried the truth but unable to deny how much she loved being around him.

He walked her to the door of her cottage and held out the case. "This belongs to your family—to you."

He bowed slightly and passed the gown to Josephine, who

had opened the door and looked unfazed by Lucy's appearance.

A warm bath was waiting for her when she got in. She soaked for a quick minute, warming up from the chill that had soaked through her bones during the walk and filled Josephine in on everything as she washed her hair.

Sleep was not an option. She couldn't even summon the will to lie down. The contents of the box might be more than she could handle, but that had never stopped her before.

At Josephine's prompting, she dressed in a pair of flowing white pants and a dark-grey sweater that wrapped around her twice and hung over her shoulder.

She knew she should run straight to Alarik with the case, or use it to bargain with Lord Daye for her freedom. But her aunt had left it to her, and she had to know what was inside.

Sneaking out, she crept to Lord Blackwell's cottage. The door was unlocked, and she turned the handle to step inside.

Moonlight illuminated his frame. He sat in a chair, alone in the dark. He looked up at her, and through the moonlight, their eyes locked and held.

Thirty-One

Lord Blackwell turned on the wall light, coating the room in a soft glow. Unlike her cottage, with a bedroom piled high in dresses and a separate space for Josephine, his was simple and clean. A dark chest of drawers had three blue-and-silver bottles on top as well as a small box for rings. The closet doors were closed, and his shoes were kept by the door.

Where were all his things? One large chair sat on a rug beside a fancy, carved end table. Lucy sat on the floor in front of the stone fireplace and set the silver case down in front of her.

"I want you to open it with me. I don't want to do this alone."

Lord Blackwell nodded, then joined her. He slowly released the lock and opened the case.

The contents looked rather normal at first glance. There were four datapads of various sizes, as well as some chips and information ports. Some looked old, others were newer models.

Lucy took out the first and lit up the screen as Lord

Blackwell lined them up and flicked through. He passed them to her one at a time, his agitation increasing.

There were multiple documents, schematics, blueprints, and dated events.

They spoke little, and an hour passed as a picture slowly formed from the bits they were able to decipher. All of these contracts and documents contained information that had not been updated in the Idex system—every mistake, some of them dreadfully dull and others bordering on criminal. And then Lord Daye's signature. The majority looked like blackmail contracts in one form or another.

Scrolling through the list of files, she noticed one with Lady Daye's name on it. Opening it, she started to read. Lucy read all the names, many of which she didn't recognize; others she did, including Henris Canmore's and Alarik's.

"What am I looking at? Is this a marriage contract?" Lucy asked. She slid beside Lord Blackwell until their shoulders touched and handed him the file.

"There's someone with answers to those questions, but he's consumed with meetings. And he's on the other side of the planet. Sorry, Lucy, there's just too much to go through. Information has been deleted here and there. We know Helix took her own information from this, and there's not a mention of her. I was led to believe this held only the secrets of a medical lab explosion twenty-some years ago, but there are other files added. I can't tell who added them. It would have had to be done manually by someone who had access. Clearly it wasn't Lady Daye or Alarik—they would have destroyed this information long ago."

"So, blackmail?" Lucy asked, voicing her suspicion.

"Looks like it. Some information was deleted, some was changed."

Lucy rested her head against his shoulder and closed her eyes. "What am I supposed to do with this? Why did she leave it to me and not just destroy it all?"

"Insurance? This must be what your uncle wants and fears. It works because, if one of them goes down, then both of them do. Evidence of Lord Daye withholding information is a crime in itself."

The door knob rattled and startled Lucy.

Lord Blackwell called out, requesting a minute as they gathered the datapads and hurriedly closed the case before pushing it under the chair.

"Open the door," Jasper's voice came as a low rumble from the other side. Lord Blackwell complied and Jasper strode in. He was out of breath and took a hurried glance between the two of them as they stood awkwardly in the middle of the room. "Lord Daye is following me and knows you went on a side quest earlier. He's already sent someone to track your speeder. It's only a matter of time before he finds you. What did you learn?"

"Madame Helix said Lady Daye was here for months before she went to the Drop—it's an abandoned observation pod," Lucy shared hesitantly, unsure why Jasper was in such a hurry to know. It had been months and months ago and was a vague clue at best. Lord Blackwell shifted his foot back slightly, nudging the case further under the chair.

"We need to leave now before Lord Daye can follow up. My ship will get us to the Drop faster," Jasper said. "No time for thinking or planning. He can't track us in my ship. How long do you think Josephine can stall for you?"

Lucy turned to Lord Blackwell; his eyes were glued on Jasper, assessing. "I'll go with Jasper if you can watch over things here?" she asked cryptically. She placed a hand on his arm and squeezed reassuringly. "Thank you for everything you've done, but I need to do this. I need to see where she went and whether she left any clues as to where she is now. Jasper needs my help."

Lord Blackwell looked down at her, his dark eyes searching hers. He covered her hand with his own and took a deep breath.

"I'll head back to the castle," he replied. "Lord Daye will likely pass me on the way, and it will take some time before he realizes we're gone, and even longer before he knows we've separated."

"Oh no, what about Helix?" Lucy asked. "He's going to find her."

"I'm sure he's not a threat to Helix, and she won't say anything she doesn't want to," Jasper said with a touch of unusual bitterness. He had one hand on the door, ready to rush out.

Lucy didn't like how fast everything was moving. She needed a minute to think, to plan. But she didn't have time—Lord Daye was coming. But was that really such a bad thing? Maybe she could use the information to bargain for her freedom.

"I need to talk to Lucy," Blackwell said, eyes like ice on Jasper.

Jasper glanced between them again. "I'll be waiting outside. Five minutes."

Lucy stepped toward the case but knew she couldn't bring it. It would be safer here. Then she spun back to the door—this was all happening too fast.

When the door closed, Lord Blackwell stopped her rapid movements and held her shoulders.

"I don't think you should go with him. I don't know what's between you two, but he can follow this lead on his own," he said. Lucy shook her shoulders a little, loosening his grip. She'd never seen him so troubled before and immediately tried to ease his worry.

"It's just the Drop. If there's a clue, we'll find it. If not, then I'll be home before my father knows I'm missing. You have what you came to Orion for. Take the case and keep it safe. Tell Alarik the truth if you get a chance, *if* he even notices I'm not with you. But regardless of what he says, I want to read all of those files when I get back. I have to see this through," Lucy said, her voice shaking with the final words. His fingers still pressed gently into her shoulders. She felt torn, wanting to take the box back to the castle, to sit and go through every page with him. To talk to Alarik—and finally tell him the truth and get some answers. But Lady Daye was still missing, and Jasper was waiting for her. She bit the inside of her lip to keep from screaming. A year of boring dinner parties and now everything was happening at once.

"I understand," he said, but the way he looked at her told a different story. He didn't want her to go any more than she did. Was it because he cared, or because he truly thought it dangerous?

"Are you going to kiss me now?" Lucy asked. She leaned slightly into his hold, wishing he would.

"I can't."

Lucy's heart sank like an anchor as a wave of sadness enveloped her. Of course he wasn't interested in her that way —he'd always been the perfect gentleman. She stared up into his dark eyes. Like the corset squeezing her chest, it was hard to breathe.

He lifted a hand from her shoulder and brushed a strand of hair away from her cheek.

"Why not? The lights are on, and I know your secrets." She felt so deflated. She didn't know why she'd asked. It wasn't as if she wanted the answer.

He traced the line of her jaw, sending an involuntary trill of pleasure down her spine.

This torture was worse than anything Evost had thrown at her.

When he spoke again, his voice was barely above a whisper, his words shaking to keep control. "I can't, because If I kiss you now, any chance I had of keeping my heart will be gone."

An earthquake was opening a chasm in her heart.

"If you leave now, I might be able to bear it," he said. He reached past her, fingers resting on the knob.

He didn't open the door.

Lucy didn't move. She didn't trust her legs to move.

He closed his eyes, as if fighting an internal battle, then released the doorknob, and tilted up her chin. Eyes searching hers, waiting for her to pull away.

"I lied. It won't make a difference if I kiss you now or not, my heart is already yours," he said finally, and slowly brought his lips down to cover hers.

The kiss was soft at first, like a morning breeze. Then came the storm that crashed into her with ferocity. She reached up and cupped his face, drawing him closer. Thoughts of him leaving her vanished. His heart was hers. He'd said so out loud, declared it. Her confusion was confronted with an intensity of longing as he kissed her.

Lucy didn't want the moment to end. If there was one thing she could do for the rest of her life without becoming bored, it was kiss Lord Blackwell. She reached up and ran a hand through his hair. He pulled her closer, deepening his kiss.

They both jumped back as a sharp knock reminded them Jasper was waiting.

"I need to go!" Lucy said, willing her legs to hold her weight. His hand held her steady for another moment before releasing her. He reached past her and she closed her eyes at his nearness, wanting very much to kiss him again. He opened the door to a waiting Jasper.

"I'll see you back at the castle," he said softly in her ear. It felt like both a promise and a goodbye.

Another breath, a step away from him. Her legs held as she left the cottage and followed Jasper.

Moonlight touched Lucy's arm as she slipped from Lord Blackwell's cottage and returned to her own. She woke Josephine and filled her in on the plan while she changed her clothing, leaving out the part about the kiss. "Lord Blackwell will need somewhere safe to work when he gets back to the castle… remember the little tower room? I'm sure it's been maintained, and I think it might be the best place."

Josephine promised she would ensure Lord Blackwell had everything he needed, all the while fussing over Lucy's outfit. Lucy wore sensible black pants and soft-black slippers with

leather bottoms. Now was not the time for elegance but action.
A hood cloaked her hair and pinned at the shoulder. When she
looked perfect for the part, Lucy snuck back out and into the
night.

Jasper led her through the trees that blocked out the
moonlight. She stumbled a few times, trying to keep up.

The ship was as black as the night, and she almost ran into
the side. When they reached the far side, a tall man stood
blocking the light from the doorway behind him.

"My name is Sers—at your service. Welcome to the
Sparrow," he said and ushered her inside.

Thirty-Two

Lucy ignored the warning in the back of her mind and boarded the invisible ship moments before the door closed. The compact ship had six seats, all trimmed in a shiny black stitching. Silver floors looked clean but unfinished, and the lights dimmed as she took a step through the open door. Taking a seat, she eyed the tall man with ruffled hair sitting at the controls. Sers wore neatly pressed beige pants and a black shirt that fit nicely.

"Where's Lavalle?" Jasper asked, sitting in the copilot seat. He sounded unnecessarily annoyed.

"Lavalle's looking for the Lark."

"What do you mean *looking for the Lark*?"

"He lost it."

"How do you lose a ship?"

"I told him the cloaking tech wouldn't hide it, and he said it would. Guess he was right. Not to worry, we won't need it until the Sparrows are finished."

Jasper looked around as if taking in the small ship for the first time.

"There's more than one?"

"We'll have five—"

Lucy enjoyed the exchange, forgotten in the seat behind them. She liked Sers and the way he poked at Jasper as if he were a child. She couldn't imagine anyone on Valtine talking to him this way.

"It's twice as fast as a dart, and you won't even feel us moving. It's undetectable. The newest model. I've been meaning to take this out for a test run."

"You've never flown it before?" Jasper asked. The two men continued to bicker. But Lucy teased out the lightest hint of sarcasm, and she wondered if everything Sers said was half made-up just to annoy Jasper.

Still, the danger sent a shiver through her arms.

The Sparrow barely made a sound. It hovered for a moment, cleared the tops of the trees, and slowly slid across the ocean until it blinked out of sight from the cottages.

When they were well underway, Lucy let her thoughts wander back to Lord Blackwell as she dozed in and out of an uncomfortable sleep. She wished she could go back and talk to him, and tell him how she was feeling.

The Sparrow took four hours to reach the Drop. As Sers had said: half the time.

Lucy was groggy from her half sleep as Jasper reiterated the plan. The Sparrow would be docked for under two minutes. He would call it back when they'd finished looking around, and he expected to be on the Drop for hours. It was quite large, and they had no idea what they were really looking for. It didn't sound like much of a plan.

"Going dark," Sers said as all lights on the Sparrow

dimmed. Lucy pressed her face close to the small pane.

As they neared, she could make out the outline of a dark mass and the soft blink of warning lights.

Lucy barely noticed a change as the Sparrow docked. There was a quiet decompress as the small hatch opened.

She stepped out of the Sparrow, her heart thundering. It had sounded like an adventure: Jasper needed help to find Lady Daye. But now that she was here, it didn't feel like such a good idea.

The dark, grey tunnel arched above their heads. Thick, scrawled panels lined the walls. Swirls and stories pressed out from the metal. Monsters swimming through a sea of stars… ships and mountains cloaked in moonlight. Lucy wondered what it would have been like to be part of creating something so long ago. It was haunting and full of life at the same time.

They reached the end of the tunnel, and a round hatch turned to easily open into a grand centre hall.

"I'll find you later," Jasper said, as he slipped past her and disappeared before she could stop him. She gaped at the space where he'd been standing only moments before.

Being alone had never been part of the plan, and yet here she was again.

Lucy looked around, wondering how she was supposed to find anything and why she needed to be involved in this part of the search. She should have asked more questions, maybe told her father what was going on. Surely he would have sent an entire team to check out the abandoned station, or perhaps he already had.

She'd been so caught up with Helix and Lord Blackwell that her thoughts had gotten away from her. This was ridiculous, and all she could do now was wander around, hoping Lady Daye had left a giant sign saying, *I went this way*. Her feet glided over the stone silently.

In the centre of the hall, she stared up at the dome. The large moon hung above them—except it wasn't really above them, it could be below them. Space was weird.

Her thoughts tumbled back to her aunt. If Lady Daye had been here, had she thought of living here? Had she been running away? Running to something? Perhaps she was scouting out the Drop as a place to host a ball—it would be spectacular.

Lucy twirled in the centre of the floor, dancing and pirouetting—making herself dizzy—when a shadow passed on the third floor.

A shiver ran down her spine, but she quickly remembered Jasper had to be somewhere. She went to follow him, to convince him this plan was ridiculous, when another sound reached her ears. She stopped moving and listened. The tinkling of a melody itched her ears, and she strained to hear the unearthly sound.

Maybe it was only her imagination, but she could have sworn she heard something.

Shaking off the feeling, she looked around to make a plan.

Metal stairs crept up three floors toward a high lookout point. The floors were a dull black rock, worn but clean. It was as good a place to start as any.

As she was heading up the stairs, movement out of the corner of her eye made her jump again. The hairs on her arms tingled, and she knew she hadn't imagined it.

On the second floor, a platform reached out, with tables and chairs set up like a restaurant of sorts. She shuddered and moved toward the tables. They were devoid of any dust or debris.

She'd never believed ghost stories, but there, alone in the dark, she couldn't control the fear of spectres and ghosts haunting the place.

"Jasper?" Lucy whispered. She knew she had heard something.

No one answered. The station fell quiet and empty again. As if it were telling her something.

Lucy pulled her hood low over her eyes, hands shaking, trying to quell the unusual wave of fear. She screamed when a hand touched her shoulder.

"What are you doing out here?" A young woman with deep brown eyes looked her up and down. She pressed her lips together in a thin line, assessing Lucy.

Lucy waited for the intense thumping of her heart to slow to something normal as she registered the girl in front of her. Recalling the time she'd come out to the Drop as a youth reminded her they shouldn't have expected it to be completely abandoned. People snuck up here from time to time.

"Oh, you scared me," Lucy said. A black eagle was tattooed from the girl's shoulder down to her elbow. At least it looked like an eagle, or a crow, but Lucy couldn't get a closer look as the girl grabbed her hand and dragged her away from the open sitting area.

"Who are you with? Don't they tell you not to leave your crew—anyone might pick you up out here on your own. And we're not supposed to be in the commons."

Lucy clutched her chest, waiting for the calm to come. The

young girl was probably in her early twenties. She wore a thick silver belt over a black top and a flashy red skirt. Braids circled a band of matching silver and held her dark-black hair away from her face. Sharp eyes set above high cheekbones assessed Lucy with a heavy gaze.

Lucy stood and stepped back from the girl.

"Snap out of it," the girl said. "What did they do? Just dump you off at the door?"

"No—well, yes, I had someone bring me here. I didn't know anyone would be here," Lucy said.

"A runaway?" she smiled, but it faded quickly.

"I thought the Drop was abandoned."

"What are you running from?"

"Marriage," Lucy said, honestly enough. "My name is… Beryl." It was as good a name as any. Her mother had used it when she made up stories at bedtime.

The girl gave her a concerned look that Lucy couldn't decipher. Then she stuck out her hand. Lucy clasped it and shook it briefly.

"I'm Em, and you're lucky—I just caught a break." Em motioned for Lucy to follow, holding a finger to her lips to keep her silent, then turned. "I have to change. Had a drink spilled all down my front. Follow me." They passed halls with floor-to-ceiling murals pressed into the metal and columns of stone with inlaid jewels.

Lucy wanted to pause and look at each one, but kept pace as Em led her up two flights of stairs to a small galley.

The office-turned-bedroom had a large desk piled with blankets and pillows and an assortment of crates, boxes, and bags littered across the floor. The view was incredible. It overlooked the main area high up, towering over everything going on below.

"I like being able to watch over everything. This is my kingdom. One day, I'm going to run the whole place myself. Isn't it grand?" Em said proudly.

Lucy looked down on the abandoned Drop and wondered what Em would say if she knew what grand looked like to her.

Em changed quickly, and without lingering, they took another pathway. Halls split off in funny angles, then always looped back around. Lucy thought they might be going in circles, but she stopped when they reached another lookout point.

Lucy watched as at least ten ships circled the Drop like black sharks.

The Sparrow had docked on the other side, hidden by their cloaking technology. If they'd been detected, it hadn't shown. But how had Jasper and Sers not known so many ships would be here? It wasn't far from Orion.

Em gave her a moment before urging her on. She led Lucy down a series of tunnels. The music grew—confirming that Lucy hadn't been hearing things earlier.

"Runaways aren't usual, so stick with me," Em said. She pushed on the heavy, black carved door, and they were hit by a blast of noise. All feelings of seeing ghosts fled.

The Drop was filled with life. A large piano crawled up the wall, and red and crystal lights hung from the ceiling. People stood against a long bar on one side. Two dozen tables or more were filled. Beyond the tables was a series of doors. It was a fully functioning station—or something.

"This place was supposed to be abandoned. How long has

this been here?" Lucy asked. For the first time, she felt a twinge of hope—Lady Daye might still be here.

"I've been here two years at least. Pretty wild. Guilds have no idea." Em bounced through the room of tables and Lucy followed.

She couldn't imagine being on this satellite for years, but if Em had been here that long, maybe she knew her aunt. "You're okay with just being here?"

"More than okay. I'm one of the lucky ones. Made myself useful. No one is here for too long. It's an in-and-out kind of place, so keep your head down. It's my turn for dishes. Just do what I'm doing."

Lucy quickly scanned the guests with wild ideas of spotting her aunt, or at the very least finding Jasper. She wondered if he'd also discovered the secret of the Drop, and if he was as surprised as she was. Everyone looked like an average guild worker; but then Lucy took a closer look. Like fast-trims or an Ambassador's scarf, there were small markings to distinguish the patrons, but Lucy didn't know what any of them meant.

The door behind the long bar opened, and Em swung inside. Following, she was assaulted by a wave of steam. The kitchen must be on the other side, as this section was only for cleaning. Em showed her the carts that carried clean items to the other side on a little belt then left her alone with the mess.

Lucy didn't mind the dishwashing, and she did her best for a few minutes, sending the clean piled dishes through the little shoot. When Em didn't return right away, she abandoned the pile of cutlery and poked her head out. No sign of Jasper or Lady Daye.

She thought about going out on her own, but the last time

she'd peeked out, she'd noticed a few men who looked less friendly and thought it best to wait, at least a little longer.

When Em finally returned, Lucy had washed and polished a tray of shiny glasses and was making a tower of sorts while the rest of the dishes piled up beside her.

"I've made a few inquiries about some of the better ships that might be looking for a maid," Em said, then immediately started washing at a dizzying speed. Lucy felt a little bad that Em was asking for her and now had to catch up on the washing. She did her best to pitch in, but her movements were much slower, and she had to dismantle her crystal tower first.

"Oh, that's very kind, but I'll be heading home soon. Actually, I was wondering if you saw someone here before. She was a lady, but might not have looked like one." Lucy went on to describe her aunt in detail, but Em just shook her head.

"Sorry, there's lots of girls who pass through here. I can't remember them all. And I know you think you want to go home, but no one goes back to Orion once you reach the Drop. What are you good at? Cooking? Cleaning?"

Thirty-Three

Lucy tried to hide her shaking hands. Of course she was going home. Jasper was here with her. The Sparrow waited, and Lord Blackwell knew her location.

A bit of fear trickled through her, bouncing from the past to the immediate present. She needed to play along, at least for now, until she found Jasper. What had Em asked? What was she good at? She had a decent list for a Valtine lady, but sadly lacked in other areas. She excelled at both planning and ruining grand balls. Lengthy dress fittings were a talent, along with spending afternoons with other ladies.

No wonder boredom consumed her life.

"I'm a great pickpocket," Lucy said at last, coming up with something and thankful to have her knife in her side pocket.

Em laughed, and after the slowness with the dishes, Lucy didn't blame her. "Everyone here says the same thing."

"No, really—I'm pretty good. Tell me who's who and I'll show you," Lucy said.

Em raised her brow, then pulled Lucy back into the crowded room. She leaned an arm casually against the wall and pointed out who everyone was, just as Lord Daye had done at the opera. People were like a web, strung together. And just like the time she'd listened to Lord Daye, the information was quickly forgotten.

Lucy quickly checked the room for an easy target. Like a ballroom, she told herself. If she pretended it was a ballroom, she could do this.

An old man sat at the bar, his long grey hair pulled back into a tight knot. The folds of his jacket were lighter than the rest from years of being creased. He drank out of a tall tankard of ale. He looked slightly inebriated and would work perfectly.

Lucy sauntered over, pretending like she belonged. She was good with people; she reminded herself. Not a group of outlaws like this, but they couldn't be much different from anyone else.

Standing at the counter, she waited and made sure she was in the right place as another man approached the bar. He wore a navy suit and polished shoes and curled his lip as he passed a table. He didn't give her a second look, but leaned on the counter. His movement naturally nudged her closer to the old man's chair.

"Oh, sorry," Lucy said, drawing too much attention to the old man. The old man checked his pockets quickly, already suspecting something was missing. Lucy took in a big breath as she slid past both of them and back to Em without so much as a backward glance.

"The old man is drunk, and an easy target," Em said, unimpressed.

"I didn't take anything from him," Lucy said, her heart pounding. In her hand, she held a small cufflink made of bright gold. It looked expensive, even by Valtine standards. "I took it off the other man."

Her voice shook with the rush of danger, and she showed Em the small bobble.

Em's eyes grew wide. "You didn't hear me tell you who he is?"

Lucy shook her head. She had been listening but not really taking anything in.

"He runs half of the trade here. The last lady to cross him got sent out on the worst trade ship. We need to find a way to get it back to him—and fast." Em's cool demeanour had changed, and Lucy tried to keep her own fear in check. Surely she wasn't in any real danger.

Lucy's mind raced, then she pulled a plan out of one of the strings of her thoughts.

"I have a plan if you trust me," Lucy said excitedly.

Em shrugged. "If it doesn't work, I'm not sticking by your side on this. I said I'd help you find a ship to work on, nothing more."

Lucy dragged her over, making a silly amount of noise and drawing far too much attention. The fancy man had a crystal glass with etched snowflakes around the edge. He traced a finger down the side. He looked incredibly dangerous, and Lucy was regretting her plan.

She stumbled back into him, thankful he hadn't noticed her the first time. Pulling Em along with her, she talked as quickly as Em did dishes. Pouring out her soul as if they'd been in the middle of a conversation.

"He's a horrible man. He's round and old, and every time I tell him I don't want to marry him, he… he… oh, what's that?

Oh, it's so pretty." Lucy stopped mid-cry to bend down. Pretending to pick the link up off the floor, she held it out to Em.

"Look what I found!" Lucy cried. Em inspected the cufflink and wrinkled her nose.

"It's fake—not worth more than a drop of haze," Em said, playing her part well.

"No way—see this crest?"

The man's attention was piqued, and he looked over his shoulder at her before he fingered his own cuffs, noticing the missing bobble.

"That belongs to me," he said, his voice menacingly low. Lucy closed her fist over it and eyed him bravely.

"Told you it has value—I bet everyone is going to say it's theirs."

Em pressed her lips together, annoyed at Lucy for not taking the first chance to return it. Perhaps she'd taken it a bit too far, but he'd never believe she was willing to give it back for nothing.

"What's it worth to you?" the man said, his voice menacing.

"Buy me a haze—and one for my friend, if you really think it's yours. She says it's worthless, but if you think it's not, then it's worth two drinks."

The man nodded to the woman behind the bar, who pulled out two glasses and filled them.

Lucy smiled victoriously and dropped the link into his palm. He walked away without a second glance. She let out a breath and quelled the shaking in her hands. She'd had enough of the Drop and was ready to find Jasper and go home. Alarik needed to be told about what was going on, and if Lady Daye had been here, surely he was more qualified to find out.

Em downed her drink, but Lucy took her time, letting the fizzing bubbles of the thick drink settle onto her tongue. She rarely had haze. She had enough ideas in her head without the drink confusing a good thought from a bad one.

Her eyes darted around the room and she realized she'd drawn too much attention—more than one person was watching her. Em finished Lucy's haze in one long swig, then picked up a tray to collect dishes and motioned Lucy to do the same. At least if Jasper was looking for her, he'd be able to find her easily.

Eventually, the leering patrons forgot about the scene she'd caused, and the room settled back into an even hum of chatter.

Lucy gathered a round of glasses, balancing them on her tray, and found she could catch bits of conversation if she kept her head down.

"Roff thinks we should hold off on the next shipment until after this summit meeting. Too many tanking ships from Valtine."

"They practically beg us to get rid of their problems."

The others agreed, and Lucy moved on, not lingering anywhere for too long. She formed a very disturbing picture as she picked up bits of conversation here and there. Most tables discussed cargo or Valtine. She heard a horrid joke about the girls being too old. Then she passed a table and connected the dots. Aside from other illegal trades, and some quite reasonable ones, the Drop was used to transport unwanted young women from Valtine or Corva to the outer planets. From what she could tell, never Orion. If they took a girl from Orion, they'd be caught. They were trafficking young women for Idex experimentation—from as young as six years old to as old as thirty.

Fear gripped her, and a line of sweat trickled down her back.

What had Em said about being one of the lucky ones? She kept her head down collecting dishes. Is this where things went wrong for Lady Daye? Why did she come to the Drop to begin with? She needed to find Jasper, needed to tell him or call Alarik.

Questions and panic made it impossible to focus. She nearly dropped her tray.

If she told Em who she was and offered her money, she could call for Alarik. Or Lord Blackwell. Surely someone would cross the stars for her.

Thirty-Four

Em was talking to someone across the room, possibly trying to line up work for Lucy. She tried to stay calm and keep herself from sprinting across the room to her. When Em stepped aside, Lucy almost died of relief to see Jasper behind her. The weight of everything rushed off her shoulders, and the knot in her stomach loosened.

He looked unconcerned and sat indifferently at a table, causing a bubble of anger to rise in her chest. She gathered a few glasses on her way over to him. If he was surprised by her ruse, his face didn't betray it. He looked more dangerous than all the men in the room combined, and she was thankful he was on her side.

She moved to his table, leaned over, and whispered in his ear, "Where have you been?"

"Did you find out anything?" he asked absently. Lucy resisted the urge to throw the tray at him.

"Yes, I found out lots of things. They're trafficking young women from the Drop, and we need to call the Sparrow and get out of here now!" Her voice rose. He was playing calm and she should too, but he was Jasper—Lord Terrington. Certainly it would be easy enough for him to get up and take her out of there.

"It's not so simple," Jasper said as if he'd read her mind. He refused to look her in the eye. "I've learned where Lady Daye went—but I had to trade for the information. I need you to trust me and not do anything rash."

His tone was ice cold. Gone was the warmth of helping her get away from her uncle. The way he was working his jaw, she saw something she'd missed before. She'd come to think of him as a friend and brother and someone she could count on. But there was a piece missing, something lacking in every interaction with him. Her mind swirled, trying to make sense of what she knew and knowing she'd never had the full picture.

"How did you know Helix told us to go to the Drop? When you came to Lord Blackwell's cottage, you already had the ship ready to go. How?" Her voice grew louder, and conversations halted to watch them. Em was nowhere in sight.

The man she'd stolen the cuff from earlier was making his way toward them. He smirked at Jasper from across the room and his eyes landed on Lucy.

"Jasper—what did you do?"

Disappointment and fear flooded her.

His eyes softened for a moment as if he was going to apologize, but he remained silent.

"I was supposed to help you find her. You said you needed me to help you find her," Lucy whispered in desperation. "What do you think she's going to say when she finds out what you did to me? You can't win her love like this."

"Who said anything about love?" Jasper pushed his chair

back and stood. The man was at her side now, and he clasped a hand over her arm. She dropped the tray, sending a shattering of glasses and plates in every direction.

Lucy turned and slammed her foot down on the man's, wishing she had Lady Cristelle's strength—or shoes. He barely flinched. With her free arm, she pulled her blade out of her pocket, spun it between her fingers, and sent it flying in his direction.

The unexpected blade startled him enough to release his hold.

Abandoning her treasured knife, Lucy ran. She sprinted past the packed tables, urged on by joking and jeers as arms reached out in lazy attempts to catch her. Someone toppled off their chair, earning a hearty round of laughter.

Escaping the packed room, Lucy darted down one hallway and then another, quickly understanding why they'd all been laughing. There were a thousand places to hide, but nowhere to go. Even if she evaded capture, home and help were out of reach.

Lucy ran down the hall, past the spires of twisted rock over the ancient floors. There was no sound of pursuit, and she slowed to catch her breath. Tears blurred her vision, and her lungs ached.

She opened one door after another, revealing empty tombs, eerie medical bays, and nowhere safe.

Lucy rounded a corner leading back to the main section again.

"Lucy!" Em called. Lucy hesitated a moment, knowing she hadn't given her real name, or perhaps she let it slip.

"Em, I need to hide," Lucy whispered, choosing to trust her

as she checked behind her.

Em's gaze narrowed, then the yelling from two floors above echoed through the chamber.

"Through here," she said, grabbing Lucy's hand and pulling her forward into one of the rooms she'd already checked. She'd been so quick, she hadn't noticed the door. It blended in almost perfectly with the silver panelling. Lucy followed on Em's heels. The door clicked behind them.

It looked like a worn servants' tunnel… big enough to carry goods from one side of the Drop to the other without being detected. Lucy breathed a sigh of relief and willed her feet to follow.

"I know this place better than anyone. No one will find us here."

They descended more stairs than Lucy could count and slunk silently through the tunnels. Any sign of her pursuers had stopped, and the panic eased in Lucy's chest. If she could hide long enough, she'd be fine.

Em ushered her into yet another tunnel, this time urging Lucy to lead the way so she could close doors behind them. When the last door closed, the darkness engulfed her. The air felt old and stale, like the regular filtration didn't reach this low.

"I can't see anything," Lucy said, feeling her way forward. The ice-cold, flat walls revealed nothing. Not a single bump, pod light, button, or decoration.

A breeze of movement tickled her shoulders, then vanished. "Em—are you there?" Lucy called. A bright light lit the interior, revealing an ancient air lock. Old enough to lack a venting system without Idex tracking or safety protocols. A large square pane of glass separated her from Em.

A decompressing hiss echoed around the room.

"I know who you are. I saw you come in with him," Em said, her voice dripping with disdain.

"Jasper?" Lucy asked. The air changed again, thinning slightly. The chamber was small and empty. It wasn't a terrible place to hide.

"He's well known on the Drop—he's killed dozens of our crew. I've been listening to the rumours for long enough, and when I turn him over, I'll be the one running the Drop."

"Killed who?" Lucy asked, shivering. "If you haven't noticed, he left me behind. He traded me as payment."

"I don't believe you! You've been lying since the second I met you, and you're working with *him*," Em shouted. "Lady Daye said the same thing. She even used the same name as you —*Beryl*. You came down to the Drop and didn't even think to use a different name? I used to work at the castle. These shippers might not know who you are, but anyone from Orion would!" Em sounded exasperated that Lucy hadn't remembered her, but hundreds of people worked at the castle.

"They aren't going to be happy if they can't find me. And if you know who I am, then you can call Alarik. I can take you with me—I'll give you whatever you want—"

"Your aunt is the reason I'm still washing dishes. Once they find out how I saved them from a trap, I'll be rewarded and put back in charge. And even *if* what you're saying is true, then Jasper sold you out, and you're better off dead. Consider this a favour."

Em left, leaving Lucy in the small hold.

Alone again, Lucy screamed and banged on the door,

searching madly for a handle.

She pried opened a small panel. Inside, a timer for the airlock release counted down. Even if someone heard her, there was no time.

She was alone with the stars.

Five, she wished she'd told her father the truth.

Four, she wasn't ready to die.

Three, she shouldn't have trusted Jasper.

Two, she loved Lord Blackwell.

One—

The airlock released and opened, pulling Lucy into space.

Thirty-Five

Instinctively, Lucy held her breath and closed her eyes as the hatch opened. Instead of being immediately sucked from the Drop, the air rushed around her, pulling her shirt in a hundred directions and compressing her at the same time.

There was a lot of shouting as someone stepped into the room, grabbed her arms and pulled her forward into the cargo hold of a ship. Her scream was swallowed by the clanging hiss of air as the door closed and sealed. The winds died immediately, and the motion plummeted her forward. She landed half on the metal floor and half on top of her rescuer.

"We got her!" Sers yelled.

"We're losing air fast," a second voice called back.

Lucy tucked her toes up to her chest, nearly kneeing the man in the chest.

Another door closed, and the hissing stopped.

She rolled off her rescuer and lay on her side.

"Hold on, it's time to go," said a chipper young voice through the comm, and before any of them could stand or right themselves, the ship darted forward, the thrust pulling her toward the wall and then evening out as their speed quickened.

Sers groaned. Getting up, he stretched his arms, then complained about young captains.

"Might need a bit more tweaking," the other man commented. He'd righted himself quickly as well and was already inspecting the back of the hull. He had a glorious curled moustache that hid a wide smile. "The seal didn't hold, and we lost a blast of air. Will need to fix it before we try flying her again."

"What do you think the problem was?"

"You don't know?"

"Of course I know. I figured it out before seeing it. I want to know if you know what went wrong."

Lucy lay stunned while the copilots argued over all the possible reasons for the seal to break and then argued some more about how to fix it. She waited for relief to flood in. She was alive. She told herself this over and over and played the moments back in her mind, but it all felt like a blank.

No fear, no panic, no relief. Taking in a shuddering breath, she squeezed her eyes tight, hoping for tears, but nothing came. She let her fingers trace the floor, the metal cold and solid, then eventually leaned up on one elbow. As soon as she did, Sers knelt down beside her. He waited for her shaking hand to reach out for his. His worn hands were warm and rough and so very real.

"That's Lavalle, so you know. You are one lucky lady," Sers said as he carefully helped her to sit. She tucked her knees to her chin and rested her forehead on them, waiting for the shaking to stop. Lavalle left and returned a minute later with a blanket.

"You don't need to get up. We can stay right here until we need to land," Lavalle offered. Lucy thanked him and wrapped the blanket around herself, sinking into it.

Jasper had left her, and yet somehow the Sparrow showed up to save her, so he must have planned it. But how could he have planned on Em trying to kill her?

"Did Jasper tell you how to find me?"

There was silence inside the cabin. Sers cleared his throat, and Lavalle pretended to hit a few buttons on a side control panel without actually compressing any of them.

"There's happenings on Orion—I'm sure your father will want to tell you about that. But someone named Lord Blackwell told Alarik where you were. Alarik called in Dr Moss, and Lavalle was on his way to the Drop before you even reached it. We met up on our primary ship and took this Sparrow instead—we've added a few new… well, never mind what we added to this Sparrow, I think you get it," Sers said. He looked as if he was ready to cry, and Lavalle continued to look busy.

Silence again.

"If Dr Moss ever sees Jasper again, he might kill him. And if we hadn't found you, Dr Moss would have killed me. The Sparrow's scanners weren't properly functioning, or we would have detected every ship out here. I had no idea what Jasper was planning when I dropped you off. Of all people, I thought you'd be safe with him. I'm sorry, little one." Sers shifted uncomfortably and patted Lucy on the head.

She'd been gone for a full day, and the only reason they'd made it to her was because of Dr Moss. In a matter of seconds, it all could have turned out differently and she'd be dead.

"So you know Jasper betrayed me? How did you find me on the Drop?" Lucy asked.

"Jasper wasn't quiet about the sale—although your name was left out of it. He accidentally broadcast it across the entire system. The Drop will be taken down within hours after the message he leaked. And finding you was a bit tricky. We can scan without loading data to the satellites, but the Drop has some cloaking in those dense walls. Couldn't get a lock on you until you were close enough to the perimeter," Sers said. Lavalle elbowed him in the ribs. "Of course, scanning abilities on the Sparrow are a secret," he added.

"It's okay—I'm great at secrets," Lucy replied, adding it to the list.

Thirty-Six

The Sparrow dropped her just outside the castle walls. It took some convincing, but Lucy assured them she would be fine and didn't require them to escort her inside.

She put one foot in front of the other, waiting for the panic or relief or something to hit her. Instead there was just a numbness she'd never experienced before.

Her black pants and hooded cloak were rumpled, her hair dishevelled—and she smelled like a combination of kitchen cleaners and sweat. But no one noticed when she entered through a back door.

Maids and butlers darted around, and there was a general sense of chaos. The whole of the castle was a hive of movement. Lucy snuck in through the servants' stairs and up to her rooms. Josephine was there, pacing back and forth. She screamed the moment she saw Lucy and ran to squeeze out whatever breath was left in her.

"What's going on?" Lucy asked as the movement in the hallway continued.

Josephine closed the door. "You haven't heard?" she asked

and immediately went to draw a bath. "Oh, I don't want to be the one to tell you." She added lavender-scented oils to the water, then rushed to Lucy's side to help her undress. Lucy struggled with the sweater and eventually freed herself.

"It's okay, Jo; it can't be worse than what I just went through."

She gasped at the bruises on Lucy's shoulder and hip. Lucy didn't even remember getting them, but it must have been when she tumbled into the Sparrow.

"What happened to you? Oh, this is dreadful. I'm sorry, Lucy. I feel like this isn't how you should find out. I know you have your differences," she paused, bit her lip, and shifted her weight from one foot to the other. "Lord Daye is dead."

Lucy stood stunned for a moment, waiting to feel, waiting for something to break through. Dead. The word didn't feel right. Still feeling numb, she sensed it hanging in the air, adding to the thick fog.

Lord Daye was dead. When? How? Jasper?

She sank into the tub and let the lavender envelop her. Josephine rushed to wash Lucy's hair.

"I don't know anything! None of us do. The Valtine lords and ladies are in a state. Staff are being called every which way. I've pulled every black dress I could find, but your father has been asking for you all day. He was yelling at Lord Blackwell about not being with you, and then Lord Blackwell told him the truth—everything. I wasn't trying to listen in, but he knows the engagement was fake now. I wish you'd been there. What happened to you?" Josephine asked again.

Lucy rinsed her hair and sloshed water all over the floor as she jumped from the tub and dried off, doing her best to explain the Drop between Josephine's gasps of horror and anger at Jasper. "I knew it. I knew it when he came to find me —when you were stuck in the corset—that there was something not nice about him. Didn't I tell you that? If I ever see him again…" Josephine brushed her hair as Lucy tied the laces on the side of the long black dress. A quick braid tied her still-damp hair back from her face.

"I doubt any of us will see him again," Lucy said and hugged Josephine tightly, promising to tell her anything else she found out, then sped through the halls.

She checked the library. The collection had increased and was spilling past the hallway. He could very well be in his rooms, but she knew he didn't like the confined space.

A portly butler walked past, stepping out of the way. He nodded at Lucy.

"I don't want to trouble you—but have you seen Lord Blackwell?"

"I saw the gentleman walking toward the south towers a while ago."

"Thank you," Lucy said, forgetting she'd directed Josephine to mention the tower as a safe space. She hadn't been up this far in years, not since she and Lady Cristelle had stolen a necklace and needed a place to hide it. Lucy wondered if the necklace still haunted the tower. It was a silly thing to think of at such a time, but at that moment, the necklace haunted her.

Her lungs ached as she took the stairs two at a time, then crossed the narrow hallway to the open door and stopped before entering.

The round room was well maintained and lined with a row of books; four long couches were evenly placed in a circle.

Luscious plants spilled out of tall planters and wound around the edges, clinging to the legs and brushing the floor. More plants hung from decorative hooks in the ceiling. The top dome was glass, and the stars twinkled in the cloudless night above her.

Small twinkling lights swirled from the floor all the way up, making the room glow, but were low enough that the lights from the village below could still be seen.

Lucy took in Lord Blackwell's frame, dressed in dark grey. He leaned against the pane of glass. One arm above his head, he looked out over the city. She imagined rushing toward him in a heap of relief—she loved him and he was so close. But as she neared, she noticed her father sitting in a large chair, shoulders slumped and head bowed.

Her stomach flopped again, like little nervous fireflies, but worse. When he spoke, she took a step back. She ducked into the alcove beside the door and waited.

"And you're sure she's safe?" Alarik asked, his voice shaking. She heard him stand and pace over to where Lord Blackwell was.

"I got word an hour ago—the Sparrows are fast. She should be back soon."

Apparently the ships were even faster than they knew; she'd been back for almost an hour already.

"This was never supposed to happen. She was supposed to be in Valtine enjoying balls and parties, safe away from all of this. Lord Daye was obsessed with his position, and I thought that ensured he'd take great care of her," Alarik said.

Lucy's heart ached for her father. He'd wanted her on Valtine where she'd be safe—that's why he'd been so relieved for her to leave and so concerned about her return.

"I'm sorry I brought her back, but it was the only way—Lord Daye was set on the engagement, and I don't know what would have happened if I hadn't played along, who else he might have forced on her."

Lucy held her breath contemplating if things had been different. What if Lord Blackwell hadn't agreed to a fake engagement? What if it had been someone else? She'd still be stuck at the midway or worse, back on Valtine with Evost.

"I should have known someone like you would have made a good match in the eyes of the Valtine court. But with or without Lord Daye's death, I would never force her to keep an engagement she didn't want. I never should have allowed the marriage between Lady Daye and Lord Daye," Alarik said, his voice crystal clear and sounding like a viceroy, not only her father. Then he softened. "Are you sure she doesn't want the engagement?"

Lucy sucked in a breath. She wanted the engagement—more than anything, she wanted to be with him.

"I think it's best for everyone if we accept that a fake engagement needs to end, and Lord Daye's death will provide a reasonable excuse."

The roiling emotions plunged through her. It was everything at once, especially the wrongness of listening in on such a conversation. She was ready to reveal herself anyway, but Nix noticed her hiding spot first, left from where he was perched near Lord Blackwell, and bounded toward her.

Unable to hide her presence any longer, she took three steps back, then noisily crossed into the room.

Alarik turned to face her. With a deep sob, he took two giant strides toward her, crossing the distance and crushing her in an embrace. Large tears rolled down his weathered cheeks, and the numbing fog lifted.

Lucy sank into the embrace, finally letting go of all the fear and pain she'd held in, and broke in the safety of his arms.

Thirty-Seven

Lucy kissed her father's cheek and hugged him again before stepping back. A guard arrived in the tower and requested Alarik's presence. He started to protest, but Lucy encouraged him to go—Lord Daye's death would create an intense stir in all of the guild plans for the summit meetings. She assured him she had to talk to Lord Blackwell and would fill him in on everything later. This was one death that would not be covered up.

"When you've finished talking with Blackwell, come and find me," he said, then followed the butler out. An evening breeze blew fresh mountain air through the open window, swaying the hanging plants. Lucy focused on the movement and brushed the tears from her cheeks, regaining control of her emotions.

"He's really dead?" Lucy asked. She knew it was true, but she still struggled to believe it.

Lord Blackwell nodded. His discomfort at their meeting mirrored her own.

"How?" she asked as she picked at the leaves of a nearby

plant.

"A delivery man found him at Madame Helix's not an hour after you left with Jasper. Heart attack, they say."

Lucy's eyes flew to his. "And Madame Helix?"

"She was out for a walk and denied everything. Her housekeeper is missing though."

"And no one thinks that is strange? Well, of course they do. Oh, I don't know what I'm supposed to feel right now. This has all been too much: first my aunt missing, and then Jasper, and now Lord Daye."

Lord Blackwell took a step toward her, and she backed up three. He stopped, brows drawn together, but gave her a bit of space.

"What happened with Jasper?" he asked, his voice coming out in a whisper. Lucy took a shaky breath and told him about Em and Jasper's betrayal. She had a hard time not crying when she confessed she'd lost his knife.

Lord Blackwell said nothing while she talked but paced angrily from one end of the room to the other. He made a fist, his knuckles straining under the contained pressure.

Lucy had never seen him so angry.

"I'm so sorry for what he did to you—" he started, then clenched his jaw.

"I need a break from all of that. I've told you everything. Now it's your turn. What did you find out?" Lucy asked, trying to ease the tension.

Lord Blackwell took a deep breath, then walked over to the open datapads that were lined up on the table. "As we discovered in the cottage, Lord Daye was involved in extensive blackmail. There are details from about twenty years ago that your father wants to tell you about. But I can share the rest. Are you sure you're up for this?"

"No, I'm not. But I need to know," Lucy said honestly. She looked out over the village, the sun setting behind the mountain. It was peaceful and calm, and felt so wrong compared to what was going on inside her chest.

Lord Blackwell motioned her forward. Her shoulder brushed his, and she focused her attention on the row of screens he had laid out.

"The security of the box allowed someone to add information yearly. There are hundreds of files Alarik wasn't aware of. They track illegal activity all over the hex-system and beyond. Instead of stopping any of it, Lord Daye was keeping the information and using it to control the Valtine courts. It also accounts for more than half of the Dayes' current estates and holdings—going back decades."

"I don't understand. Who was adding information? Lord Daye never left Valtine."

"I don't know, but I think Alarik does. What I can't figure out is how Lady Daye got the box."

Lucy hesitated for a moment, then mentioned Wynter's lack of Idex, which filled in the last pieces for him. It explained why the lab explosion twenty years ago was still being kept a secret.

"Did Lord Daye know the box was missing?" Lucy asked. It didn't add up. Lord Daye never worried about Orion. His secrets were here, but he never was, not until now.

"He would have been notified if anyone unauthorized entered the room. Alarik naturally had concerns about the security box, knowing its original contents, but no one was allowed in that room or near the desk unless approved. Not a single alarm was triggered, not even once. My family are representatives for Alarik's side on the contract. Lord Daye must have learned about my involvement, which would explain why he wanted us to marry. Having his own representative, and then me, married into the family would give him unconditional control."

Lucy paced the room. Trails tugged at the corner of her mind, bits of information she had tucked away. Things Helix had said.

"What did my Aunt need the box for? And is the Drop mentioned at all?"

"I don't know. The updates stopped about four years ago, and I have no idea what Lady Daye and Madame Helix deleted. There are backup mechanisms for the backups. I'm still working to retrieve it, but it'll take some time."

Lord Blackwell's family had been working with Alarik—she should have known. He'd never once lied to her, but she still wished she'd known. And she was no closer to finding Lady Daye—if anything, that hope was further away than before.

"I think I want to sit alone for a while," Lucy said, taking one of the heavy knit blankets from the window seat. She climbed up and tucked her knees under her chin, watching the lights in the village blink out as evening fell. Lord Blackwell began to pack everything up, but she stopped him. "But I want to be alone with you, if you'll stay with me. You always like sitting alone in the dark, and I think that's what I want right now too."

Lord Blackwell turned all the lights off, leaving only the moonlight, then sat behind her on the long window seat. Nix, who'd taken to spending his time with Lord Blackwell in the tower, curled up at his feet.

Lucy shuffled back until she could rest her head on his chest. Taking a deep breath in, she embraced the moment. She was home, and safe. She had a few more days to pretend to be engaged to Lord Blackwell, and she would take whatever she could get before having to end it.

He wrapped an arm around her and let the darkness steal away the pain.

Thirty-Eight

Mourning would last three days, but Lucy didn't feel like being sad for Lord Daye. She slept, ate, and dressed, then spent the day in the tower with Lord Blackwell, combing through all the information while the world around them thought she was grieving.

Lord Daye had ruined families through fear in order to gain more and more power. Over decades, Lord Daye had increased his hold on land titles for the secrets and errors of many who weren't even alive to bear the shame. She wished he could face trial—instead of resting in death.

When they discovered his connection to the Drop, it was worse than either could have imagined.

The recovered data was undeniable and yet still so incomplete. Whoever was uploading information to the secured box included damning details implicating Lord Daye, perhaps blackmailing him in return. It was information that made her stomach turn. Accounts and ledgers couldn't be denied. Lord Daye had been sending children away from Valtine. She knew he had been cruel, and rambled constantly about Valtine perfection, but to send away "imperfect" girls made Lucy want to throw up. If he'd known what Lucy knew that they were being used in experiments to unravel the Idex coding—perhaps he wouldn't have sent them. Underneath those files was another layer of notes Lord Blackwell was trying to dig up. The strands of coded and lost information left out Lord Daye but indicated that Lady Daye was complicit in the trafficking. She'd been a part of the crew that had tried to stop the experiments twenty years ago, so why appear to be helping them now?

But if felt impossible to deny. Lady Daye had known about the Drop; Jasper was willing to risk everything in his hunt for her and the stolen information; and she had known to disappear without a trace.

Lucy left Lord Blackwell to continue his work and went to find her father. There were so many questions, and Alarik held the answers.

As promised, Alarik flew her to the spot where, over twenty years ago, everything began.

After all of the stories, Lucy expected to see charred remains and a pile of rubble. Instead, the ground was even. Polished stone covered the entirety of it.

Levelled they'd said. But Lucy should have known better— secrets didn't go away. They just went underground.

Alarik led her to a wide stairwell that dropped into the mountain. The walls were marked with ancient stories pressed into the metal, each telling a tale that led into the next. They descended into the mountain, and Alarik began his story.

"I was already married to your mother, and we were living

comfortably on Orion when all of this happened. Your mother was a Valtine lady but was in poor health and not permitted to live on Valtine—not that either of us wanted to. When you were only five years old, both of my parents died within a month of each other, and as you can imagine, Lady Daye couldn't handle it. My father's death was not even mentioned, and then after our mother passed—there was nothing. No way to say goodbye. Death was ugly and imperfect, and Valtine doesn't accept mourning. We brought Lady Daye—who was only sixteen at the time—to Orion. Your mother tried to comfort her—but Valtine was in my sister's blood. She couldn't cry, couldn't break away. That was when I promised your mother I'd never let you be raised like that, even though your mother owned her own vast estate on Valtine. Lady Daye was sixteen, so much younger than myself and more of a big sister to you than an aunt. She quickly made friends here, and I thought Orion was good for her."

They entered the stale labs. All traces of medical equipment had been removed. The tunnel was polished stone, and it reminded her of the Drop, with the carvings on the walls. The same familiar feeling flooded over her, like she'd been there before.

"She got mixed up with Helix and Henris and Domo. I knew some of what was going on, but she was young, and I couldn't imagine her getting too involved. There were always rumblings and a lot of discontent within the guilds over Valtine and Idex control."

He took a deep breath in and paused to admire the imprints on the walls before continuing.

"The group was split over some of the experiments. Henris

and Madame Helix, along with others, agreed the human experiments crossed the line, and when the others refused to end the work, a group led by Henris decided to take out the lab themselves, erasing any trace of their involvement. You were always sneaking out as a child. As you can imagine, your Idex was easily tracked. That night you followed your aunt."

Lucy touched the walls where the scorch marks blackened a massive stone ship. At the end of the hall a room opened, and she went inside. Nothing but bare walls and floors. The end of the line. Beyond that, the hall was sealed, and Lucy knew that beyond there, the rubble from the explosion remained. She said nothing, imagining her six-year-old self following her aunt despite the dangers.

"Lady Daye didn't know you were there, and you couldn't keep up. We found you wandering the mountainside. I was going to take you back home, and your mother was going to find Lady Daye, when the lab exploded. She ran in, and pulled out as many people as she could. By the time I reached her, she'd breathed in so many toxic gases. Her lungs were already weak, and she didn't survive the rest of the year."

Lucy reached to hold his hand. She couldn't imagine how difficult it was for him to say all these things to her because she knew hearing it felt like a thousand knives stabbing into her heart.

"How does Lord Daye fit into all of this?"

"He came in, a charming senior lord of Valtine, and promised to clean up the mess. He knew all the right things to say and how to make it all disappear. We had an agreement. Your mother's lands were officially transferred over to Lady Daye instead of to you. He hid the proof that would destroy

Lady Daye and so many others. The guilt Lady Daye felt over your mother's declining health and your narrow escape overshadowed everything. She begged me to allow her to marry him and make it right. A contract was made that, in one year, she would marry. In order to guarantee both parties kept their word, the box was designed to hold all the information, but with it—Lord Daye's admission of covering it all up to get what he wanted."

They stood in the empty room, and Lucy could almost picture the devastation that night had caused.

"Two years later I was made Viceroy."

"Because of Lord Daye?"

"No, because I told the guilds about what really happened and the information I had." Alarik flexed. "They applauded Lady Daye's sacrifice to keep so many of their own Orion guilds safe. The files were vague and were closed without all the details. It was a tragic accident. But not everything could be erased—Wynter and the other survivors, for one. The box was moved to the safe room in the castle, and if anyone in the party went into that room, we'd all be notified. Security was set up around the desk, allowing for cleaning and staff. A third party was brought in to have access, to prevent a breach in contract. Lord Blackwell's family was the one listed for our side."

"And who was on Lord Daye's side?"

"The captain of the Obsidian." Alarik said the name with disdain. Lord Blackwell's earlier assumption that Alarik knew who was regularly adding information was correct.

"Captain Ward's uncle?"

"As a representative, security need not be flagged when he

entered the room. Then he died unexpectedly."

"That happens a lot around Madame Helix," Lucy murmured.

"Yes. But his demise, I believe, was natural. It does happen sometimes."

Lucy raised a brow. It was insane that so many turned a blind eye to the deaths.

"Captain Ward was never informed for the obvious reason of his impeccable character. Lord Daye had yet to set up a new partner, but it didn't matter. Lady Daye must have had a reason to steal it—I just wish I could ask her what it was, and why she didn't come to me first."

She placed her hand on her father's arm and squeezed reassuringly. There were so many times she should have come to him first too.

"I never should have let her marry Lord Daye. I won't have you marry Lord Blackwell for the good of the family name."

"Well, the engagement is a problem for tomorrow. Today we decide what to do with the contents of the box—the ones added after the explosion." They made their way from the stone tomb and into the daylight. Birds chirped overhead, and blossoms poked up through the short grass. Spring air filled her lungs with just a bit of hope that all would turn out well.

"There are dozens of Valtine families on Orion right now who are being controlled by Lord Daye—they will be afraid of what happens now that he is gone. I can make my recommendations to you, but you are the only heir, and the courts will not accept my word. There will also be fear that the contents of the box have leaked," Alarik continued.

Lucy thought of the general chaos back at the castle and

wondered how many travelled with them from Valtine out of fear. It should have been a hard decision to give up her status as a Valtine Lady. Lady Cristelle was taking on both the guilds and the court and wielding her power. But she came by it honestly. Her father had built the Inkton empire, and her lands on Valtine truly belonged to her. For Lucy, there was no question of keeping or maintaining power. "I want to give them their secrets back. Anyone who is carrying the weight of someone else's mistakes needs to get their information back quietly. One family was paying Lord Daye to keep a dead grandfather's affair quiet. Anyone who is being controlled for utterly ridiculous reasons needs to be freed," Lucy said definitively. "That will take care of the bulk. Honestly, the things people let control them is absurd to me. The rest—the names of the missing girls, the families who sold them, and everyone on the Drop—I want it made public at the summit meetings."

Alarik looked down to the village. "Secrets keep us safe," he said, but for the first time there was uncertainty in his voice.

"Perhaps for a while they do. But if everyone knows I have Lord Daye's secrets, then I'm not safe holding them. And who knows, maybe more people would be willing to do something if they were given the chance. Maybe we'd care more about missing girls and less about the colour of our shoes at an evening ball if they were given the truth to care about."

Alarik turned to face her. "You look so much like her."

"Like my mother?" Lucy asked.

"No, like your aunt twenty years ago. She was so determined to keep everyone she loved safe."

"I think she knew," Lucy said, smiling up at him. "When she

left the box with Madame Helix, I think she knew what I would do with it."

"This is dangerous ground we're walking on, and you are going to expose some very dangerous people. And you won't be able to return to Valtine after Lord Daye's scandal is exposed"

"What does Dr Moss think?" Lucy asked casually.

"I see nothing gets by you," Alarik said, then changed the subject.

"So that would be a no to answering questions about Dr Moss. That's fine. And I don't want my inheritance on Valtine. I'm certainly not even the rightful heiress to the rest. What truly belonged to Lady Daye can sit the required ten years for all I care. All the excellent staff who are currently doing a wonderful job can continue—which reminds me, I need to add a few names to the list to be employed. I'll tell you about that another time."

Lucy and Alarik walked arm in arm into the sunshine and the promise of spring. But there were still so much ahead of them, and Lucy wasn't sure if she was ready to be the one to sort it all out.

Thirty-Nine

Two weeks later, Lucy met Lord Blackwell in the tower for the final time. He was setting the last items back into the locked case.

In a short time, they'd dismantled the Daye empire that had taken decades to build, and yet the remaining assets would still constitute one of Valtine's largest landholdings. Rumours of the boxes contents spread quicker than the truth did. Some of the Valtine court fled to the outer planets, the ones who knew they would be exposed at the summit meetings. Some returned to Valtine to reclaim lands. Most planned to stay for the duration of the meetings.

"Do you think Lady Daye knows her husband is dead?" Lucy mused, looking out the window. Shuttles flew in and out of the hub. Dinners and parties would be where the real exchange of information happened—the summit meetings would only formalize it all. Tonight was the first ball of the pre-summit meetings, and it was the formal event where she would end her fake engagement to Lord Blackwell.

"News of his death will reach the outer planets fairly quickly.

If she doesn't know yet, she will soon."

"If she's alive," Lucy said sadly.

"I hope she is. I uncovered this," Lord Blackwell said softly and handed her the datapad.

Lucy held up the screen and scrolled through, reading as fast as she could. It was the information Lady Daye had deleted and Lord Blackwell recovered.

"Is this what I think it is?" Lucy asked, her throat constricting. It was the last piece. Everything made sense now. Why Lady Daye had left, why she'd risked everything by going to the Drop, and why she'd given Lucy control of what remained.

"Do you want to tell everyone the truth?"

"Yes, I'd love to—but not all stories are mine to tell. Thank you for finding it for me." Lucy held the datapad to her chest, hoping and believing Lady Daye had made it. "Is there any way to tell Jasper?" she asked.

"I could talk to Dr Moss and see if we can locate Jasper, if that's what you want." Lord Blackwell crossed his arms over his chest and held Lucy's gaze. She nodded, then held her breath. This was the final thing for them to do, and then it was all over.

"I guess this is the end of things, then," Lucy said, waiting for him to repeat what he'd said at the cottage and assure her that none of the secrets they'd uncovered in the past two weeks mattered. But looking at the datapads, she knew she couldn't ask that of him. She'd so clearly renounced her own position on Valtine that, if he married her, the scandal of her uncle would no doubt reach his sisters. He had people to protect, and her life was on Orion. She'd known this moment would come, but she wanted to stretch it out a little longer, to spend just one more day with him—and then another and another.

"Yes, I suppose it is," he replied. Placing the datapad in the container, he closed the lid of the box. The only items remaining were from the explosion twenty years ago. He sealed it shut and handed it to her. Alarik would have it reinstalled in the office where it would stay until all of this work was over.

Lucy wanted to ask him to kiss her just one more time, but he didn't move toward her, and she didn't know how.

Leaving her heart in the tower, she brought the case to Alarik and then made her way to her rooms where a glorious surprise awaited her.

"I can't believe you're here!" Lucy cried as she hugged Lady Cristelle and Wynter—and then Lady Cristelle again since she hadn't hugged her properly the first time. Lucy hurriedly tossed dresses and shoes from the chairs so they could all sit down. "But why are you here?"

Wynter hung a dress over the bed rail and sat down. She looked confused. Lady Cristelle kicked aside a random shoe and poured them all tea before taking a seat across from her, equally perplexed.

"We're here for your wedding. Why would we miss it?" Wynter asked carefully.

Nix pawed at the wedding dress box from Helix that had arrived earlier. Lucy hadn't opened it. She didn't need to.

Taking a sip of tea, she looked from one friend to the other and burst into tears. Through sobs and cupcakes, Lucy told them all about Lord Blackwell from the lambs to the corsets and everything after. Lady Cristelle paced and Wynter knelt beside Lucy, rubbing her back.

"I still don't understand why you aren't marrying him," Wynter said for the third time.

"Because even if he loves me, he can't put his sisters at risk. He declared his feelings at the cottage when we kissed, but since then, nothing has happened. We both agreed to end the engagement. He said himself that it was best."

"Not everyone says what they're feeling," Wynter replied and looked down at her hands as if she were keeping a few secrets herself.

"I do." Lady Cristelle took a small cake from the pile, earning a glare from Wynter. "Fine—Wynter is right. Why would he share his feelings for you? Look at it from his perspective. From what you've told us, he was super dreamy in the study but never wanted to deceive you into doing something you wouldn't want to. He admitted then that he wanted to kiss you. You told him you would never marry a Valtine lord and reiterated it every chance you got. You were seen leaving a garden maze with Lord Ryon, covered in grass stains, and you leapt at every chance to be with Jasper, eventually trekking after him to your almost-death. This after finally kissing the man who's literally followed you across the stars." Lady Cristelle really had a wonderful way with stories. Wynter looked at Lucy expectantly.

"You think I'm the reason he hasn't declared himself for me again? Because he thinks I don't love him?" Lucy asked, looking between her friends.

"Yes," they said in unison.

"You don't think he's worried about his sisters' reputation?" Lucy asked, taking a sip of the scalding tea. She set it down, her heart fluttering with hope, but needing to hear it from her friends.

"He's still pretending to be engaged to you, isn't he?" Wynter said gently.

"He would have broken it off the first chance he had if he was worried. Instead, he spent weeks sorting through secrets and cleaning up the mess Lord Daye left behind," Lady Cristelle said, a little more directly this time.

"I should probably go talk to him," Lucy said, still feeling a little stunned.

"You should probably finish getting dressed first." Lady Cristelle eyed Lucy's dressing robe as Wynter held up the yellow gown she'd brought for the evening.

"I helped Clair finish it for you," Wynter said.

It was another soft-yellow that Wynter had brought especially for the event. Like sunshine, the lace hugged her curves and swept over her hips before reaching down to her toes. Wynter started to fasten the jewels to the back clasps, but Lucy was impatient and decided every other clasp would do the trick.

"I brought you something, as well. I designed it especially for your wedding, which may or may not happen now," Lady Cristelle said, holding out a small iridescent vial. Lucy opened the bottle and breathed in the beautiful scent. It reminded her of jasmine at night mixed with something sweet and fresh. She dabbed a small amount on her wrist and ran a brush through her hair, then picked a tie off the table and sped from the room, tying her hair up as she ran.

Reaching his rooms, she knocked on the door. When no one answered, she made for the tower. Lucy raced up the stairs, out of breath.

"What's wrong?" he asked, the moment he laid eyes on her.

The lace caught on the door when she stepped forward. As she tugged, a light tear stopped her in her place.

"Everything is wrong. I love you, so give me three reasons I shouldn't marry you. No, give me one good reason for calling off this engagement," Lucy said and tugged again, trying to free herself. He crossed the distance between them and knelt down to pull the lace ribbon from the hook. "Tell me you hated the lambs at the ball and think I have dreadful ideas. Tell me you despise space travel, and we can't make this work. Tell me you're not interested now that I'm no longer going to inherit vast lands. And I know I just gave you lots of reasons we shouldn't be married, but tell me none of them matter. Please tell me what you're thinking."

He raised a brow and stood. Lucy couldn't read his face. Her heart squeezed, and all the air rushed out of the room.

He wasn't talking. He needed to say something, or she might lose her nerve.

"In time, you'll regret being married to me. Jasper might have betrayed you, but we both know there were reasons, and if you'd followed his plan, he might have had a way to keep you safe. There's still hope Dr Moss can find him. I won't stand between you two and that is a reason I cannot bear," he said, holding up the bit of ribbon.

Wynter had been right. Lucy's mouth hung open for a full two seconds before she snapped it shut. She took the ribbon from his hand, wishing she could re-do every moment of the last two weeks and show him that she'd cherished every second with him. How she hadn't been thinking of Jasper—or nursing a broken heart.

"This is what happens when I talk too much—everyone misses the important parts. I love you. And I'll say it again and again so you know that every second I spent with Jasper, I was dreadfully bored. I never once had any feelings for Jasper, other than anger. But with you—I could spend the rest of my life with you. Even when we're not saying anything at all, it is positively the most exciting part of my day."

The ribbon hung between them, swaying back and forth. Lucy resisted the urge to yell at him to say something or grab the ribbon back and run away. Her dress slumped off her shoulder, the clasps not holding together, what with the rush in which she'd dressed. She pulled at the sleeve, desperate to keep the dress together.

"Turn around and let me help," he said finally. She turned her back to him, her heart ready to burst and shrivel up at the same time. He pulled her hair back and knotted the ribbon around it to hold the curls in place. Then he freed the half-knotted laces from their hooks and reset them one by one. Tying the bow, his hand rested on her shoulder and sent light dancing to her toes.

He kissed the side of her neck, and her world stopped spinning.

"I was enthralled when you brought the lambs into the ballroom," he whispered and kissed her just below her ear. "I was enchanted with you when I pulled you off the wall. And I fell in love in the dark. Neither of us is tied to Valtine in any way that matters. There are no reasons for me to want to end our engagement."

He kissed her shoulder again, and Lucy's heart felt like it

would burst into a thousand suns that fell as quickly as they rose.

"Oh no!" she cried, stopping his kisses. Turning, she buried her face in his chest. "The dress. You're going to marry a truly hideous bride! And Wynter! I can't believe what I did to the sweetest of friends."

How was she going to explain the dress? Lord Blackwell had told her to reconsider before she signed the contract, but the consequences had seemed so far away.

"I don't care what you're wearing, Lucy—as long as you're mine."

Forty

"I'm sorry I did this to you," Lucy said, holding Wynter's hands in her own.

Wynter Canmore wore a subtle rose-coloured gown. Pink crystal roses glimmered against black lace. The young seamstress had a talent for blending in. Lucy wondered what it was like to be barely noticed, then decided it was better left to people like Wynter.

Lucy's stomach dropped. Her wedding gown truly was ugly. Red and brown streamers curled from the waist, and ruffled layers billowed at her chest, both flattening it and making it bubble in an unflattering direction. Hip pads bounced when she walked, and aqua-blue fast-trims adorned the bottom.

"I signed the contract when marriage felt impossible. We were on an adventure looking for my aunt, and it didn't matter what it would do to your reputation because it was never supposed to happen. The contract says I can't even marry in private. There was a guest minimum. And it doesn't even matter if she can't attend, the contract is ironclad. I'm so sorry. I'll make it up to you."

"But you do? Want to marry him?" Wynter asked.

Lucy's smile spread across her face, and she bounced, making the hip pads wobble. "Life certainly surprised me—but, yes. I want to marry him."

"Then don't worry about the dress or my reputation. I already have more than I could ever want. And I have you as a friend. Besides, I was already thinking of giving up the shop and maybe travelling—getting away for a bit until things calm down. This might give me the excuse I need to leave the shop to Clair. She's great."

Lucy sobered. *Until things calmed down,* meant never. Since releasing Lord Daye's blackmail information and reverting lands back to their rightful owners, there'd been a frenzied rush to maintain control. And Wynter's lack of Idex made her an evident target. It was only a matter of time before the wrong people confirmed her identity.

"No matter how far you travel, you will always be a dear friend. One I don't deserve. And no matter how ugly the dress, I still look fabulous."

"You look radiant," Wynter replied. They stood side by side, looking in the mirror. Lucy had never been more excited—or dreaded anything more—in her whole life.

"No one could make this dress fabulous, but it feels good to say it."

Wynter did her best to make sure the dress would stay in place, then left to take her seat in the grand hall. She was about to become a mockery among the Valtine court and guilds alike, and yet she went inside to celebrate her friend's wedding. Lucy didn't deserve a friend like her.

Alarik came up behind her and groaned.

"Never make a deal with a guild woman—those contracts are like iron. I read it over three times. What were you thinking?"

"Lesson learned. And I was thinking I couldn't possibly ever get married. I never thought I'd love someone the way you loved Mother."

"Lord Blackwell is a good man. And there are many kinds of love. I imagine your mother's and mine would have changed and grown over the years."

"You look handsome. Hardly seems fair."

He kissed the top of her head and took her arm.

Lucy took a deep breath, squared her shoulders, and put on her most dazzling smile, hoping Lord Blackwell's family didn't despise the sight of her.

Alarik nodded toward the footman who stood at the end of the hall.

He reached up and plunged the hall into darkness.

"What's going on?" Lucy asked. A butler passed her a small coil lamp.

It barely illuminated her feet.

"I wasn't the only one who read over the contract. Your future husband looked it over, too, and found a bit of a loophole."

The grand doors opened to the great hall. The blacked-out ceiling didn't allow even a hint of sunshine to peek through. Glow lights held by the guests flickered like fireflies, illuminating faces and hands.

The guests saw nothing more than her glowing lamp and the small span between her hands—and perhaps a hint of lace. Her dress might have been a mere corset, and no one would have known.

Alarik led her down the aisle, his steps steady and sure. She squeezed his hand and let him guide her. Her full heart pounded in her chest, and she let the small tears fall.

She stopped where Lord Blackwell stood, holding up a coil. She turned and hugged her father tightly, then took Lord Blackwell's hands.

Without waiting for the ceremony to start, he put an arm around her waist, pulled her in close, and kissed her.

Blushing, she took his arm and walked up the final three steps toward her future.

The Drop

Wynter let her feet hang over the edge of the third-floor
balcony, looking down to the unaware co-pilots below. She had
not yet been formally introduced, but Cristelle and Lucy had
both given her a colourful description.

"Are you sure you want to bring this stuff with us?" Sers
asked, nudging a long hose with his boot.

"This is one of the best filtration systems ever created. Do
you know how old these are and how hard they are to find?"
Lavalle responded, holding what looked like a filter bag close to
his chest.

"You already have two on every ship."

"These parts are worth their weight in gold."

Wynter watched the two pilots bicker back and forth,
enjoying the moment. She leaned back, sighed and took in the
ceiling's beauty, its large dome displaying the stars above. The
Drop was ancient. She couldn't help but wonder if her family
had worked on it. If a brother had pressed the intricate designs
into the cooling metal, or if a sister had visited, excited
with the possibilities of the space observation pod.

Now it was truly empty.

The illegal operations were shut down days after Lucy had

been rescued. Dozens had been arrested, and dozens more escaped. Cleaning teams had scoured it, and then it was locked up and closely monitored by routine patrols.

Not that the increased security mattered to Sers and Lavalle.

The storm rolled in as Dr Moss approached the pilots, his shoes thundering on the ancient stone floors. A hush fell over the now-abandoned Drop, and Wynter had to strain to hear their words.

"I have our course set…" Lavalle said, as Sers picked up the additional parts off the floor.

"How bad is it?" Sers asked.

"Alarik has the hex-system distracted with summits, and I've delayed my plans for returning to the Obsidian. Lucy has done more in three weeks than any of us could have hoped to accomplish in decades. But whatever you thought you were prepared for—it's worse," Dr Moss replied, then he looked up to where Wynter was perched.

"Time to go," he called to her.

Wynter slowly stood, running her hand along the decorative metal banister as she made her way down to the main floor—each step taking her away from her past and into the unknown.

When she reached the bottom, Sers and Lavalle had piled their treasures onto a cart and were walking ahead. Dr Moss stepped over a dropped end piece. Wynter picked it up and tucked it under her arm, giving the men a wry smile as she followed them out of the grand hall and down one of the docking tunnels.

"Last chance if you want to stay here," Dr Moss said to Wynter.

"I've already said my goodbyes," Wynter responded and

lifted her chin. It wouldn't be forever. Six months, maybe a few more. The hex-system wasn't safe for her anymore, and Dr Moss could use her help.

Dr Moss raised an inquisitive brow.

"I left a note," Wynter corrected softly, then stepped past Dr Moss and onto the Lark.